DRACO DAWN

COLIN DEAN

In memory of Graeme Keel—
a great friend and fine fisherman.
"Tight Lines"

Acknowledgements:

To my poor suffering wife, June,
and my children, Helen and Robert,
who have had to put up with my
constant Roman "Do you know" facts.

TABLE OF CONTENTS

PART ONE:
CORNELIUS FUSCUS

CHAPTER 1:
The Stronghold, 87AD

The carrion crows, once surviving on meagre scraps of waste, now ravaged their deadly feast of festering limbs and torsos. The birds, free from intervention, picked and jabbed at the corpses with their deadly beaks.

Titus Livius Decimus lay among the dead and dying, injured and pinned by the sheer weight of the fallen. He struggled to remember how long he had lain there. The putrid smell of drying blood and expelled bowels filled his senses, making him retch and gag. As his consciousness slowly returned, disbelief of his beleaguered situation hit him hard.

Only days before at Vadin-Orlea, he and 20,000 comrades of combined legions, including his own Legio V Alaudae, had crossed the rugged Dacian Iron Gates Gorge. Carved by the mighty Danube River over thousands of years, the gorge split the Balkan Mountains to the north and the Carpathian Mountains to the south. Over two months, the Roman force had built a floating pontoon bridge, surmounting the mighty river. Using strong rams fixed on ships and handled by pulleys, the engineers and legionnaires had driven down huge wooden pillars two rows deep into the river bed. Like a wooden centipede, it stretched a thousand metres between both banks. Titus Livius marveled at the Roman ingenuity and engineering skills. No effort was spared to create any project. In this case, a bridge to allow the transportation of thousands of men, horses, and equipment across the river. A secure platform to start their campaign to defeat the Dacian tribes.

Titus Livius remembered how the excitement grew and spread throughout the "Castra" as news reached of the orders to prepare to break camp. Each individual cohort commanded by their leader, the "Pilus Prior," seamlessly undertook their strictly rehearsed routines. Breaking down tents, carefully packing tools, each man preparing his own equipment pack and weapons, ready for the forthcoming campaign. Steadily, they formed, cohort by cohort, organised and precise, until all five legions were prepared to move. Ever confident in their inevitable success to follow, the Roman war machine set forth.

A seemingly endless tide of disciplined soldiers moved in synchronised rhythm across the wooden bridge, penetrating the early morning mist that silently shrouded the structure. The steady rhythm of thousands of sequenced **caligae** (Roman military sandals) on timber created a deep, resonant drumming echoing across the water. Each cohort seamlessly combined to create its own individual legion, moving as a single sequenced entity. Marching ever onward, fleeting glints of gold sparkled from armour, as rays of sunlight broke through the fading gloom.

At the forefront, standard-bearers proudly held aloft the eagle standards, the symbols of Roman power and unity. Behind them, ranks of legionaries, their faces stern and determined, carried their gladii sheathed at their sides and large rectangular shields slung over their backs. The centurions barked orders, their voices cutting through the rhythmic march, ensuring order and cohesion as the legion advanced.

Cavalrymen led powerful warhorses, the animals' hooves clattering on the wooden planks. The horses, draped in protective barding, snorted and stamped, their breath visible in the cool air. Wagon trains creaked under the weight of supplies, groaning under the load of equipment essential for sustained campaigns.

Engineers stood vigilantly, monitoring the bridge, their faces etched with concern. Wooden beams, reinforced with iron and secured by solid stone abutments on either side of the river, groaned and creaked under the massive weight it was sustaining. But still, the bridge held firm.

Behind the infantry and cavalry, streams of auxiliary troops followed. Their diverse backgrounds evident from the group's varied equipment and attire. Cretan Archers mobile, accurate, and deadly, with ornate bows and quivers slung over their backs. Their firepower and menace increased the Roman army's missile capability in the field. Men tall and lythe, cloaked in bright orange tunics, proudly carrying their painted spears. Both groups shared a common bond. Their conquered provinces, now part of the empire, jointly contributed their unique skills to Rome's might.

As the army in its entirety crossed the bridge, their purpose was obvious. This was the march of an empire. A superior force that would imprint its unstoppable will in whatever manner required upon its Dacian enemy. The bridge itself seemed to sag under the weight of destiny, carrying not just men and materials but the ambition of Rome stretching ever forward.

Titus Livius, at twenty-seven years old, had proudly marched across the bridge in uniformed sequence amongst the throng of men. By his side, "Lakon," his trusty companion, trotted, happy to be free of the camp and once again on the move. Lakon was a Canis Molossus "dog of war." Covered in scars that protruded through his jet-black, short, dense fur, he stood thirty-two inches to his massive shoulders and neck. Weighing over one hundred and twenty pounds, he carried this mass with an air of power and agility. His head was the most defining feature, broad with a pronounced muscular jaw and a short but deep muzzle. Eyes dark and alert, they exuded a calm but watchful gaze, continually assessing his surroundings.

Lakon was a true titan amongst dogs, built for strength and bred to guard or spearhead full-on attack. He was a formidable force of terror, yet to Titus Livius, he pledged absolute and unwavering loyalty and trust.

The day drew on, and slowly, the masses crossed the bridge. The air was filled with the mingling sounds of clinking metal, creaking wood, and the snorting of horses. Distant calls of officers, barking orders and cajoling men onward combined into a symphony of excitement and purpose. Unforeseen issues often hindered the orchestrated flow. A metal rim around a cartwheel ripped free. The now unbalanced cart violently lurched to one side, and with a final decisive *snap*, the wheel detached completely from the axle. Spinning wildly away from the cart, it uncontrollably careered along the bridge toward a cohort. Five men had to dive off the bridge into the river, with the wheel smashing into a second cart and up-ending it. The force of the impact spilled the precious contents over into the river.

A horse, agitated by all the activity, was further spooked by a sudden horn blast. Eyes widening and nostrils flaring, it kicked and bucked. Driven by instinct, it attempted to bolt. Only the quick thinking of a cavalryman, who threw a cloak over its head and grabbed its bridle, restrained it before it could gallop through the masses, causing mayhem and injury.

As the late afternoon sun slowly dipped into the west, the main body of the column finally reached the safety of the rivers margin. The advance party of engineers, who had crossed as part of the initial vanguard, had been establishing the layout of the secure foothold for hours. Scouts who secretly crossed the river at night in small boats over the last two weeks had steadfastly produced detailed maps and reports of the terrain ahead. They identified the best position, reconnoitered materials, and outlined pitfalls. Their secretive labours enabled advanced knowledge of where and how to proceed in constructing the critical military camp.

The chosen site was situated on a slight elevation just beyond the river bank. It provided a strategic vantage point, using the Danube at its rear as a natural defense. Of the three unaccounted sides, two were facing immense, almost impenetrable forests, offering ease of access to the trees required to build the camp. The front opened up to a rough path barely two carts wide, enabling the only approach forward. Now, with the main body safely on the north bank of the river, the vast Roman legionary force set its sights on establishing a secure foothold.

The camp followed the standard Roman rectangular design, in this case, a quarta castra: a practice honed to perfection over the centuries. Built to precise measurements, it provided a clear hierarchy of practical working and lodging space. Engineers and surveyors expertly marked out the perimetre, indicating where the ditch and wooden fences would be positioned. All around the encampment, thousands of legionnaires began digging the defensive ditches, each fully aware of their role played in the camp construction.

Whilst they dug, a host of legionnaires were deep in the immense forest that surrounded the camp, hurriedly cutting down trees. Axes were being wielded, and huge two-man saws were being pulled across the freshly felled timber, fashioning the fifteen-foot wooden palisades. Each end of the posts was axed into a point ready for use in the fences. Cart horses pulled the posts lashed together in groups of six, hauling them along the full length of each perimeter ditch. Here, they were drawn up and positioned, ready to form the defensive wooden wall. The resultant overspill from each job was never wasted. Earth, from the excavation of each ditch, was in turn used to build a rampart, reinforced with stakes and wooden palisades.

The interior was divided into zones with the streets laid out in a grid pattern. At the heart of the camp sat the **Principia**, the headquarters, where the commanding officers, standard-bearers, and scribes gathered. Cornelius Fuscus, the Praetorian Prefect, sat at his desk, staring through the door of his tent at the rapidly growing castra. It resembled a small city, with thousands of figures methodically carrying out their assigned roles with clockwork precision. Throughout the camp, he could hear and see the urgency to complete construction. His officers barked orders, chastised the slow, and cursed at any delays. Engineers carefully ensured that the establishment of the key stanchions were positioned correctly and vertically. Thousands of legionnaires working in disciplined organisation heaved, sawed, and hammered, creating the wooden palisades.

The last glimmers of sunlight scattered across the darkening sky, as fingers of light danced amongst the slowly encroaching dark clouds. Shadows grew longer, on the wooden palisades, silently rotating eastward as the sun fleetingly hovered and finally slipped below the horizon in a blaze of reds and yellows.

Cornelius Fuscus smiled to himself as he watched the outer walls rise on all sides at an astonishing pace. Secure perimeters already taking shape, providing safety and assurance for the entire camp. It was, undoubtedly, an overwhelming testament to Roman organisation and discipline. An unparalleled display of their ability to project power deep into enemy territory.

The camp's front gates, the last part of the perimetre, were finally being hauled into place. Huge blocks were positioned either side to allow each door to be suspended upon them. On either side, guard towers were being constructed. The sound of hammers, saws, and axes filled the air with a constant rhythm as Titus and Lakon walked slowly past the watch towers into the camp.

The camp was alive with sound and smells. Fires were lit, and the smell of cooking rations filled the air. Soldiers were meticulously pitching leather (papillo) tents, in strict alignment as designated in the castra plan. Eight legionnaires organised into a contubernium, each sharing a designated space within the tent to house a wooden chest for their personal belongings. Weapons and armour, gladius (sword), pilum (javelin), scutum (shield), and lorica segmentata (armour), were carefully placed either near their sleeping mats or stacked outside. This strictly enforced order and meticulous efficiency, whether in temporary or permanent camps, ensured the legionnaires were battle-ready at a moment's notice.

Just as Titus turned to make his way to his tent, a call rang out from Centurion Sextus Aemilius. "Report to the Praetorian Prefect on the double," he said. "Make sure that fucking dog doesn't shit in his tent."

Titus smiled and instinctively patted Lakon's head, while the dog, in turn, intuitively lifted his leg against a cartwheel.

As Titus ran towards the Principia, he could now see soldiers standing guard at the completed pallasades. Standing on the raised inner wooden ramparts, their eyes scanned the horizon for any sign of enemy movement. Along the ramparts, racks of Pilums were strategically positioned, providing ease of access to mass weapons if attacked. Outside, in front of the palisades deep in the ditches, a crisscross of sharpened six-foot poles provided a deathly barrier for any would-be attackers. The defensive barrier, only rough fields and trees hours ago, was now a functioning curtain of safety for the legions.

Titus was distracted from his route by shouting and screaming coming from the back of a line of tents. He could hear men's voices and what appeared to be a younger man pleading his innocence. As he turned the corner at the top of the line of tents, he could see in the distance three legionnaires and one young lad. The largest of the legionnaires, who appeared to be a monster of a man, had his back to Titus and was beating and shaking their contubernium servant.

"This will teach you to be a thieving little bastard. I know you have taken my leather belt," he said.

The servant, now in tears and bleeding from the nose, cried out, "It wasn't me; I haven't been near your things."

This only incensed the soldier more. He put his enormous right hand around the lad's throat, started to squeeze hard, and lifted him slowly off the ground. The lad started to gasp, his legs kicking in spasm as his breath failed him.

The quietest whistle left Titus's lips. A black shadow sprung forward, like a cougar, hitting the ground and closing the gap on the unseeing group within seconds. Lakon took an enormous leap and hit the legionnaire, strangling the lad. All one hundred and twenty pounds of power and muscle hit him straight in the middle of his back, knocking him completely over and releasing the lad from his deadly grip. It all happened in a split second.

The felled legionnaire, initially dazed, got to his feet, growling and cursing, "Who the hell was that? I'm going to kill whoever the bastard is."

Lakon stood his ground, growling, whilst watching the two other soldiers carefully. One of the soldiers shouted, "Fabius, stay still. It will rip your throat out."

The servant, who by now had caught his breath, scrambled behind the back of a cart, hidden, watching intently.

Titus arrived on the scene and signaled for Lakon to back off. Lakon slowly walked backwards, still growling, and stood obediently by him.

Fabius pulled himself upright and said, "Is that fucking dog yours, because if it is, you and it are dead?"

He was a giant of a man, with a jagged scar that carved a path from temple to jaw. Broad as a battering ram and grounded like an old oak, his frame was built for war. Hardened by years of brutal battle, Titus was left in no doubt, Fabius was a battle-scarred veteran of countless campaigns. He wasn't about to let anyone ruin his fun.

The reason for beating the lad was forgotten now; he had been embarrassed in front of his friends, and he wanted blood. Fabius took a step forward, his fists clenched, his eyes fixed steadfastly on Titus. He had broken men far bigger than this throughout his life, and he had no fear. He steadily advanced to his next victim.

Titus gave a second longer whistle. Lakon moved away and stood in front of the two soldiers, steely-eyed and gently growling. His intention was totally clear to both men. They stood still.

Titus stood his ground, rolling his shoulders and gently twisting his neck. He raised his fists, stance shifting slightly. He awaited the attack.

For a big man, Fabius was quick! He lunged, swinging a huge fist straight for Titus' jaw. The younger man slipped to the side, just enough to let the blow graze his cheek. He countered with a quick, solid jab to the ribs. Fabius didn't flinch! The man, toughened from years of battle and street fighting, just laughed. Instantly, he kicked Titus straight in the knee. His knee gave way, and as he fell backward, a solid uppercut followed through, glancing off his shoulder and dampening the force.

Titus grunted and tried to stand up. The knee held, but it was going to slow him down. Fabius came again, this time lunging with a powerful straight jab before driving a brutal left hook into Titus's stomach. The air rushed from his lungs, and he again stumbled back, gasping, trying to find some space. Fabius knew he had his man; he had won hundreds of fights, and this was not going to be any different.

Titus was hurt; he had to think fast. As Fabius came at him, he spun away, baiting him into stepping forward. At the last moment, Titus shifted his stance and delivered a sharp elbow to the older man's temple. Fabius staggered, but instead of retreating, he surged forward, grabbing Titus by the tunic and slamming him against a wooden support post. He slumped to the floor.

Fabius now prepared the killer blow! He pulled Titus's limp body up by the hair, held tightly in his enormous fist. He drew back, his right arm ready to slam his fist straight into the stricken man. He smiled; he could see the final act already.

The face exploding, the senses leaving the man and as he dropped, the brutal kick to his head, finishing him completely. *Then I'll kill that dog!* Fabius thought.

Titus tried to gain as much purchase as he could from the wooden post he was held against. His vision blurred, it took all of his strength to focus. Fabius moved forward but saw the flicker of movement too late. Like a viper, Titus reached forward, jamming his straightened fingers deep into the eyes of his combatant. Instantly blinded, Fabius screamed. He dropped Titus and fell to his knees. He held his hand to his face as dark red blood poured through his fingers. He would never terrorise the camp again.

Titus pushed the stricken man onto the floor as he limped over towards the remaining two soldiers, both in a state of shock and held by Lakon's fierce stare.

"You two," Titus said. "Take him away and get out of my sight. If I hear of any bullying again, Lakon will not be restrained." He whistled again.

Lakon released his stare, immediately moving to Titus's side. The young servant, who had watched the fight safely behind the cart, crept slowly forward, totally shocked by what he had witnessed. He had tears streaming down his face, and his lips and nose were still bleeding from the beating he had taken. Lakon quickly turned and growled at the noise behind him, constantly protecting Titus. On closer inspection of the servant, he decided there was no threat and sat, staring at the dejected human.

Titus gently asked, "What's your name? How long have you been beaten by that monster?"

"My name is Gaius Flavius," he said. "I have been assigned to his contubernium for over a year."

Titus looked carefully at Gaius Flavius. On further inspection, he could make out multiple scars up his legs and arms, and chunks of hair were missing from where he had been constantly dragged.

"Well, you are safe now," said Titus. "We will find you another contubernium to support."

Gaius burst into tears again and hugged Titus.

Titus responded, "In the meantime, come along with me; you look as though you need a good meal."

Titus, with his face bloodied, bruised ribs, slowly limped on towards the Principia. Faithful Lakon, as always, walked by his side, constantly vigilant. Gaius, like a shadow, walked a few steps behind them both, still dazed and shocked by the change in his circumstances.

Titus although broken, still had orders to meet Cornelius Fuscus.

CHAPTER 2:
Trouble Brewing

Night had fallen as Titus, Lakon, and Flavius arrived at the Principa. Although late evening, they were met with a scene of constant activity. Soldiers, officers, and support staff purposefully engaged, each playing their part in maintaining the efficiency of the camp.

The Principa was more than just a headquarters—it was the very nerve centre of the legion. Decisions were made, orders issued, and the fate of thousands of men's lives could be decided in a moment.

At its centre stood the **Aedes Signorum**, the sacred tent housing the **aquila**, the legion's revered standard. The tent, adorned with banners and insignia, conveyed an atmosphere of solemnity, reflecting the importance of the eagle to the legion. Titus could just see the golden eagle glinting in lamplight through the gloomy tent. Four legionnaires were posted to guard the sacred deity. Two either side of the standard, two guarding the entrance. Menacing, alert, eyes ever-watchful, they scanned for any threat to the sacred standard.

To the right of the *Aedes Signorum*, the Praetorian Prefect Cornelius Fuscus had his tent positioned. An opulent yet functional command centre where Emperor Domitian's most trusted officers held counsel.

Speculatores, the Praetorian Prefects personal guards, mirrored the Aquila Guards, protecting the entrance. Alert to unwelcome intrusion or attack, they vigilantly monitored all movement. If necessary, they were ordered to put their own lives on the line and offer the ultimate sacrifice.

High-ranking tribunes and centurions constantly reported, their faces lined with the weight of responsibility. Scrolls detailing intelligence, troop movements, and supply lines lay scattered across an old wooden campaign table. Stained with candle wax and blackened it had served its purpose well.

Fuscus was clad in his lorica segmentata, and a purple-red cloak was draped over his shoulders. His seniority was displayed for all to see. He was tall of stature, square-jawed, with bright, enquiring eyes. Although in his mid-forties, he still had the physique of a hardened soldier. Daily combatant sessions with his Praetorian guard ensured his sharpness and maintained his fitness. Often, they retired wounded or just conceded to his aggression and swordsmanship. He was not just a stab-and-thrust legionnaire; he possessed skill, posture, and cunning. A Roman officer not to be crossed. His men followed him without hesitation and with unwavering loyalty.

Fuscus was a proud man from a proud family. They were part of the *equites* (cavalrymen) property and social-based classes of ancient Rome. Rich, powerful, with enviable influence. Second in social standing only to the senatorial classes. As a member of this exclusive equestrian order, all doors were open to an ambitious man.

He embraced all possible connections, every path that could lead to success, no matter the cost. During the "Year of the Four Emperors" civil war in 69 AD, he first distinguished himself as one of Emperor Vespasian's most ardent supporters. Advancement and ambition were always uppermost in his mind. His defection from Emperor Vitellius in favour of Vespasian's cause was a master stroke. His fiery zeal and passion gave Vespasian's movement the stimulus and momentum it required to succeed. Fuscus' own cause unquestionably benefited, too.

His bravery and leadership led to him becoming Vespasian's commander, leading the Legio V Alaudae legion in the invasion of Italy. When the second most senior fleet of the imperial Roman navy, "Ravenna" a counterpart to the Praetorian Guard also defected to Vespasian, it was Fuscus who was appointed as commander.

With the death of both Vespasian and his son, Titus, Domitian, the youngest son, became emperor. Cornelius Fuscus proudly accepted the role of Prefect of the Praetorian Guard, a post he still embraced now six years on!

Two years prior, in 84 AD, the Dacians, led by King Decebalus, crossed the Danube into the Roman-controlled province of Moesia. Burning, killing, and wreaking havoc, they captured the Moesian governor Gaius Oppius Sabinus, tortured and killed him. The Dacians continued their onslaught, ravaging the province burning and destroying forts along the Danube. Emperor Domitian, outraged at their impudence to Rome, immediately launched a counteroffensive. Domitian personally traveled to the region, amassing a huge force, once again commanded by his trusted Praetorian Prefect Fuscus. The Dacians, experts in Guerrilla warfare tactics, put up fierce resistance over eighteen months but were eventually successfully driven back across the Danube.

Domitian promptly returned to Rome to celebrate his greatness, parading before the Senate and the Roman public. An elaborate triumphant parade, full of pomp and glory, portrayed him as Rome's great warrior.

Fuscus, on the other hand, was left by the Danube. Domitian had given him strict orders: Annihilate Decebalus and remove the threat of Dacian Tribes forever!

Titus, Lakon, and Gaius started to walk towards the Prefects tent. A mass of soldiers, auxiliaries, and servants were constantly crossing the open square, making their passage across difficult. As they tried to cross, the sound of galloping horses rose above the cacophony of the square. It came from the direction of the camp gates, steadily increasing in volume as the horses drew nearer. The crowds suddenly parted as three mounted scouts surged into view amid a cloud of dust. One legionnaire, too slow to move, was violently hit in the back. He spun away, smashing into a cart full of Amphora's containing oil. Slowly, he dropped to the ground, unconscious and bleeding profusely.

Titus was close to the horses; he could see their eyes wild with fear and mouths dripping with foam as they angrily pulled against their bits. They were covered in sweat and had been ridden hard! One of the scouts had a long gaping wound down his right arm and across his thigh. He struggled to stay upright on his mount, slumping forward across the horse's neck. Blood surged from the whole of his right side, covering the flanks of his horse like a shining red cloak.

The other riders, both ashen, clearly required attention to multiple smaller wounds. Auxiliaries rushed to restrain the horses, holding their bridles tight, whilst others helped each scout to dismount. The scout, with the gaping wound, was put onto a wooden stretcher, and four servants carried him straight off to a nearby medical tent.

The two remaining scouts pushed aside helpers, shouting, "Get out of the way."

The surrounding crowd quickly moved aside as they ran towards the command tent and disappeared inside. In seconds, loud voices could be heard from inside, followed by violent banging of fists on the wooden campaign table.

Thirty minutes had passed when the heavy leather tent flaps were thrown open. Centurion Sextus Aemilius stormed out. Sextus suddenly spun around, grabbed Titus, and said, "What the fuck are you doing hanging around outside here? You were ordered to the Prefects tent an hour ago." He then took a second look at Titus and spat out, "By the gods, what horse kicked you? What good are you if you can't fight? Get your arse into that tent now and leave that bloody dog outside."

Sextus Aemilius was not a man to ignore. The Roman army ran on fear of the centurions, and at thirty-eight, he was the most feared in Legio V Alaudae. As a centurion, it was not good enough to just be a good soldier. You had to have a combination of skills and physical attributes. Big, strong, intelligent, and literate, all whilst being an unquestionable killer. A centurion fought on the front line with his men, leading and conveying orders. Survivors of years of combat, they slowly worked their way up the chain of command.

Life expectancy was low. Sextus Aemilius was an exception; only the best survived. He led, he disciplined, he taught—all edged with a streak of arbitrary cruelty. The *vitas* (vine branch) he had been presented with on his promotion to *Primus Pilus* (First Spear Centurion), the highest-ranking centurion and leader of the first cohort, was not for display. Of his cohort of four hundred and eighty men, the majority had personally felt it. The rumours were that it was an inch thicker in places due to the layers of skin stuck on it. His job was to cloth, feed, organise, and ensure they were all fit and ready to do their duty. Sextus Aemilius' cohort was always exemplary!

Titus quickly saluted. Sextus looked at him with disgust, turned and rushed away. He was clearly more occupied with urgent things rather than lashing out. Titus ran over to Lakon and Gaius, who were waiting by the side of the Prefects tent. He said, "Gaius, wait here and keep a low profile. Lakon, you stay." As he said it, he laughed to himself, "Keep a low profile with a monster like Lakon by your side."

He turned and marched quickly back around the side of the tent and straight up towards the entrance. The two Speculatores guards looked at him with true Praetorian rancour. One of them said, "What the fuck do you want?"

Titus confidently said, "I have been ordered by the Prefect to meet him."

Without a further glance, the nearest guard to him said, 'Wait here, don't move." He turned with precision and disappeared back into the tent.

The remaining guard looked at him with total disdain, coughed, and then spat a huge lump of phlegm down towards Titus's sandal.

The first guard quickly returned with a look of atonishment on his face and said, "He will see you." He growled then, "Proceed."

Titus smiled. Pulling himself upright, he marched past the guards into the oil lamp-lit gloom of the command tent.

Cornelius Fuscus stood dictating orders to a scribe who was feverishly writing them onto wax tablets. Fellow clerks and scribes equally laboured in the outer administrative tents, sitting at wooden desks cluttered with wax tablets and bronze styluses. They managed the legion's records, supplies, and correspondence. The might of Rome thrived totally on structured order!

Fuscus looked up and saw Titus standing by the entrance. The inner sanctum guards were blocking his path through to the main command centre with crossed spears. Fuscus raised his hand, and instantly, the guards withdrew their spears, opening the route. Titus walked onward, greeting his Prefect with a clenched fist across his chest whilst formally saying, "Ave."

Fuscus acknowledged him and gestured to follow him to the back of the tent. He pushed back some heavy red curtains, opening up an entrance to a smaller meeting area. The space had a small table, two chairs and an old, worn brass oil lamp that barely pierced the dark. A small pool of oil lay around the base of the lamp, slowly seeping into a brass holder.

Once both men had entered, Fuscus roughly pulled the curtains across, shutting out the noise from the main tent. "Take a seat," he said softly.

Titus sat down opposite him and studied the man. He exuded power, confidence, and breeding. Fuscus pulled out a chair and then slowly sat down. He folded his arms and said, "Roman gold outshines the sun."

Titus looked Fuscus straight in the eyes and instantly replied, "The moon will fade when the Draco dawn arises!"

There was a moment of silence between them. Then, the two men smiled.

Fuscus asked, "How is that barbarian Decimus Cornelius Balbinus"?

Titus laughed and said, "Alive and still as hard as nails."

"He wishes health to you."

"*Tibi salutem dico.*"

Fuscus laughed and said, "That man will live forever; eternity flows through his veins."

Titus's mind drifted back to how he had first met Centurio Exercitator, Aulus Septimius Balbinus – Master Trainer of Legions.

Titus' father, Marcus Livius Decimus, had served in the Legio X Gemina for twenty-eight years and retired as a gnarly old Centurion. On his retirement, he was awarded one hundred and fifty thousand sesterces and a large plot of fertile land in the hillsides of Hispania. It included an ancient olive farm requiring a lot of repairs, although allowing him to establish an annual income and hopefully prosper.

Marcus had been a soldier all his life. He had seen the world and fought many battles. Whilst many had died, he had survived. He was a proven leader, respected and feared. Yet, with all his experience, he had never run a business or, indeed, a home. He decided that his best plan would be to buy a slave housekeeper to run the home. He could then concentrate on rebuilding the farm.

The heat of the July sun was beating down as he walked through the old town, heading towards the slave traders' quarter. Many traders had set up their auction stands conveniently situated around the harbour. Men, women, children. Africans, Gauls, Germans, and all nations from every part of the Roman Empire were available for sale. Some for domestic service, some for farm labourers and the most expensive for the gladiatorial circus.

A cacophony of voices resonated loudly around the square walls. Traders pitched, "Look and see, powerful legs, good teeth, strong back."

"Come, check; mine are the best you can buy."

Marcus absorbed all the sights and sounds as he slowly walked the stands. He was unaccustomed to market traders and didn't want to be tricked or taken for a fool. He had worn his centurion's armour. Forbidding and intimidating, the traders grew wary of him and allowed him to look at their stock in silence. As he visited the fourth stand, he saw standing at the back, a beautiful woman with long black hair. She was tall and lithe and stood proudly with an air of indifference to all.

Markus walked over toward her. He carefully looked her up and down, felt her arms, and went to feel her leg. She pulled her leg backward angrily, glared fiercely, and spat at him. The trader whirled his long wooden switch and went to beat the woman. His arm was swiftly held in a vice-like grip, totally unable to move. The next moment, he found himself on the floor with a huge sandal pressing down on his throat.

Marcus menacingly growled, "Drop it."

The trader was choking and started to turn blue in the face. He immediately let go of the switch, waving his open hand vigorously to prove it was dropped. Marcus hesitantly released the pressure. A torrent of swearing came from the trader as he got to his feet, sensibly putting some distance between Marcus and himself.

There was something that drew the woman to Marcus. Strong, confident, and defiant. If he didn't end up with a knife in his back before the week was out, he felt she would be perfect to run a strict household.

"How much?" said Markus gruffly.

"Seven hundred," came the reply.

Markus smiled and then carried on walking.

The trader ran after him but still kept a healthy distance away. "Six hundred and fifty," he said. "The best I can do."

Markus didn't stop.

"Alright, Alright, you drive a tough bargain. Six hundred, and I'll throw the bastard in, too."

Markus stopped and turned around to the trader quickly. "What bastard?" he said. He looked over to the woman, and there, standing and holding her leg, was a lad of about eight. A replica of his mother, dark black hair with fierce proud features.

Marcus looked at the pair, both staring defiantly at him. He thought it through. He could do with a young pair of hands to help him with the farm. If the boy lived and grew, he would be able to help him in his old age. Marcus turned to the trader and said, "Let the agreement stand."

The trader responded, "So be it."

Marcus reached into a pouch on his belt and handed over the money.

The trader walked over to the woman and child, unlocked their chains, and passed a rope to Marcus that was tied to their bound wrists. Marcus looked at the titulus around the woman's neck. It listed:

- *Age: approx. 25*

- *Skills: Cook*

- *Origin: Dacian*

- *Known defects: Wild*

Marcus led them both through the noisy market streets. He went out through the old west gate to where he had tied up his oxen and cart. He threw a few coins at some local boys who were protecting it and grabbed the reins. He loosened the ropes and went to lift the woman into the cart. She shrugged her shoulders away, kicked Marcus hard, and promptly climbed up into the cart by herself, pulling the child firmly behind her.

Marcus laughed out loud. He tied them both onto the back of the cart, walked to the front, and hauled himself in. As he flicked the whip, the oxen let out a low moo and slowly pulled the cart forward. Marcus turned and looked at the woman and smiled. Her face like thunder, she spat again, then picked up an old ear of corn and threw it at him. He faced back toward the road, still retaining his smile. Was he imagining it, or did all those men turn quickly to see her walking beside him?

Marcus freed the boy and his mother from slavery after three years of their purchase. He married the woman and adopted the boy as his own son, naming him Titus. Good food, fresh air, and exercise allowed Titus to grow up strong and healthy.

Marcus insisted on a regimented life, instilling the values of his military service years upon Titus. He was educated and taught how to fight and ride a horse like a cavalryman. Hours of swordplay ensured discipline, precision, and the art of survival.

At the age of eighteen, Titus had presented himself to Aulus Septimius Balbinus, Centurio Exercitator – Legio X Gemina with a letter of recommendation from his father.

....

Centurio Exercitator

I, Marcus Livius Decimus, Centurion of Legio X Gemina, respectfully present my son, Titus Livius Decimus, a Roman citizen of good standing, for your consideration to join the ranks of Legio X Gemina.

Having reached the age of service, he is eager to offer his strength, loyalty, and skills in the defense and continued glory of Rome. Titus possesses a keen intellect, is trustworthy, and is well-versed in the art of reading and writing. Under my guidance, he has trained rigorously with the gladius, pilum, and scutum, following orders without hesitation. In addition to his martial skills, he is an adept horseman and excels as an athlete.

His ambition is to serve the emperor with honour, to prove himself on the field of battle, and to safeguard the noble ideals of Rome. If accepted, Titus shall devote himself fully to the values and traditions of Legio X Gemina, pledging his unwavering obedience to your command and his life to the legion and the eternal city of Rome.

May the gods bless you and grant favour upon Rome.

Marcus Livius Decimus

Centurion, Legio X Gemina

....

Aulus quickly read through the letter, then put the wax tablet down on his desk. He stood up and slowly walked around Titus, assessing the man before him. He had heard great stories of Titus's father. He was revered and a legend in the legion. He had once single-handedly fought his way through to an isolated signifer – "Bearer of the Signum," standard of the century. Although wounded, he dragged the signifer back to the ranks, saving the man and the signum. The pride of the century was secured.

The Centurio Exercitator returned to face Titus. Aulus was built like a battle-hardened warhorse. Piercing dark brown eyes stared out of his scarred, rugged, tanned face. A long scar down his right arm was a testament to past battles.

Aulus nodded, smiled, and said: "Titus Livius Decimus, I will personally recommend your Dilectus. You will be a fine addition to the legion."

Instantly, his right knee went straight into Titus's groin. On impact, Titus bellowed out, his head involuntarily pitching forward. Aulus hit him hard, straight on the chin. Titus crumpled and sunk to the floor, barely conscious. He looked up through watery eyes as Aulus stood over him. His uniform was adorned with vividly colored circular battle pendants, each a testament to his valour on the battlefield.

Aulus spat on him and growled, " You are now the lowest of the fucking low. Don't think that just because your father was a legend, you will be treated any differently than any of the other useless bastards I have to turn into legionnaires."

Aulus stepped over Titus and walked to the door. He roughly pulled it open and shouted, "Optio, get this piece of shit out of my office and put him in the reception hall. He is ready to swear the Sacramentum. He will be perfect for twenty-five years of service."

Cornelius Fuscus' voice summoned Titus sharply back from his thoughts, "I am told you are Aulus's most trusted and elite Frumentarii."

"The news we have just received from the Scouts has just made your assignment harder."

Fuscus briefly glanced down at the small lamp burning on the table, then looked back at Titus and said, "Decebalus has massed thousands of tribesmen in Tapae. They are a proud race and will stop at nothing to defend their lands and protect their gold."

Fuscus stood up and walked over to a cabinet in the corner of the tent. He opened up a small drawer and pulled out a wax tablet; the seal of Emperor Domitian was clearly emblazoned on the outside. He spoke quietly, "Here are your orders direct from Domitian." "Prepare yourself. We break camp tomorrow."

Fuscus jumped to his feet, pulled back the curtains with an enormous swipe, and shouted, "Summon the officers and centurions. I have orders."

The bugler immediately ran outside the tent and blew three long blasts, followed by a short one. This signal was repeated throughout the camp by fellow buglers, ensuring that every officer and centurion would hear and urgently respond.

The whole command structure of the legion had presented itself in the command tent, anxious to hear why they had been summoned so late in the evening. The rattling of lorica segmentata could be heard amongst the many voices of the men gathered. At the far end of the tent, Fuscus was briefing an orderly whilst signing off an order. Titus had slipped past all of the main body of the crowd and had positioned himself by the exit, ready to slip out once Fuscus had made his speech.

Fuscus finally stopped his briefing, turned around, and took two steps forward toward the men. There was no nervousness or sense of concern; this was a born leader who was on his stage. He picked up a glass of wine from the side of his desk, drank a large gulp, coughed, and then said, "Gentlemen. Today, we stand upon the edge of destiny. Roman steel shall carve vengeance into the bones of our enemy! To a man, we shall bear witness to such triumph that our names will be written on giant columns of honour in our beloved Rome.

"The Dacians, like cowards in the dark, have committed unspeakable treachery, striking down our own governor. His blood cries out for justice, and it shall be delivered by our swords!

"These savages, lurking in their cursed mountains, have dared to defy the might of Rome. They do not fight as men should with discipline, courage, and the strength of a soldier's oath. No! They skulk like wolves in the night. They think their mountains will protect them. They believe their Gods and shadows will save them. But no, Roman fire will burn their forests, Roman might will break their strongholds, and their warriors will know what it is to die at the hands of legionnaires. There will be nothing but ash and their widows will weep for those who dared to oppose Rome!"

"Fight, not just for vengeance, but for the honour of the empire. It is the will of Emperor Domitian himself! He has set his gaze upon Dacia, and we are the instrument of his desire! Through our strength, Rome shall prosper!"

"The Dacians will not expect mercy; none shall be given! We shall take their land, their gold, and their very legacy—and in its place, we shall raise the banners of Rome!"

Fuscus then raised his voice to a shout. "SO, SHARPEN YOUR SWORDS, STEEL YOUR HEARTS, AND MARCH FORWARD WITH ME TO TAPAE. TOMORROW, WE FIGHT FOR SUPREMACY! WE FIGHT TO REMIND THE WORLD THAT ROME NEVER FORGIVES, AND ROME NEVER FORGETS!" The tent resounded with a tremendous cry " For honour and for Rome."

The night was short! The whole camp was awake and moving before a cockerel crowed. Across the castra, all of the contubernia were fully engaged in the tasks of preparing food and breaking camp. Each of the eight men, along with their servant, was organised and ready to undertake his assigned role. Lighting a fire, preparing food such as wheat, cheese, and olives. Filling water bottles, feeding and readying the animals, they laboured to strike their tents and pack the carts. A hive of activity, their efforts followed routines regimented throughout Roman military history.

The night before, Titus had found Gaius a placement in a new contubernium. They openly welcomed Gaius and his services, as their previous servant had been killed in a tragic accident. He had been crawling under the cart, trying to retrieve a box that had fallen underneath. A pair of oxen had been spooked and, in their panic, dragged the cart forward, instantly killing him.. When Titus checked with him, Gaius was happily serving the team.

Titus was preparing to feed Lakon. He was sitting on a discarded wooden amphorae container, left as firewood for the remaining camp guards. He had a large bowl of raw meat, topped up with leftover scraps and sprinkled with garlic to enhance strength and aggression. Lakon pushed his mighty head into the bowl and, with great gulps, demolished the food. He then proceeded to push the bowl around, trying to lap up the last little bits. Finally, he stopped, looked up at Titus and barked.

Titus reeled back, chuckled, and said, "Lakon, if your bite doesn't kill them, your breath certainly will."

What had been a small city was now rapidly becoming just four wooden walls. The Aedes Signorum sacred tent that housed the legion's Aquila standard was packed and loaded. The Command tent and administrative tents were already in a large cart, moving slowly down the camp, being drawn by two oxen ponderously moving forward. Any lumber that could be used again was loaded, ready to be hauled. All that was left was a small guard contingency, who would remain and protect the stronghold.

Rome was on the move. Thousands of marching feet, horses trampling, carts rumbling, banners flying, and the standards at the front, proudly shouldered by signifers. Surely, a sight to put fear in any enemy!

Titus stood up and slowly looked around the emptying camp. The steady cadence of the departing legionaries echoed off the timber walls as they marched onward towards Tapae. Titus smiled at the unmistakable sound of power. Then the stench hit him. Twenty thousand men, open latrines, horses and cattle. It hung in the air, foul and unrelenting, a reek born of humanity and beasts. A parting gift for Dacia from its soon-to-be master: Rome.

He no longer thought the remaining guards had been given the easier detail. Titus wondered if the Dacians' reconnaissance was able to sniff out the enemy camp from afar. It was time for him to move out quickly!

Titus reached into his leather loculus, which contained his most important possessions. A small hand knife his father had given him when he left home. Treasured wooden gods, Janus, guardian of thresholds and change, beginnings, and transitions; Minerva, she who governs reason and the art of war. Pride of place was a handmade amber talisman made by his mother. It was on a small chain, too small for him now, hollowed out. A number of strands of her jet-black hair were contained within. She had died when he was fifteen. Titus always felt her presence when he held it. Besides these items, there was the wooden wax tablet he had been given by Cornelius Fuscus.

He pulled it out and re-read the orders. *"By Order of: Imperator Caesar Domitianus Augustus Germanicus, Pontifex Maximus, Tribuniciae Potestatis XX, Imperator XXII, Consul XVII, Pater Patriae*

Titus Livius Decimus

I have been assured by my most trusted Centurio Exercitator and Primus of Speculatores, that among all his men, you stand as his finest—a whisper in the shadows, ghost in the dark, the last noise before death.

The Dacians, like cowards in the dark, have committed unspeakable treachery, striking down our own governor, Gaius

Oppius Sabinus. His blood cries out for justice, and it shall be delivered by our swords!

It is my command, my will, that you infiltrate their ranks, unravel their secrets, and sow terror in their hearts. By guile, by fire, by pain—make them tremble, make them weep. Discover their gold mines, the very veins that sustain their nation. Unearth the means to break them.

We fight to remind the world that Rome never forgives, and Rome never forgets!

Go forth and make them kneel."

Titus slowly closed the wax tablet. He knew Fuscus had secretly opened the sealed orders. His speech the night before had contained verbatim some of *Domitian's* words! He walked to a fire burning nearby and dropped the wax tablet into the centre. As it burst into flames, the message, which meant so much more than the few lines of text, bubbled and melted away into the ashes.

He picked up his pack, walked over to the horse he had sequestered from Fuscus's stable, and carefully tied on his belongings. An expert horseman, he swung himself up into the saddle, gathering the reins into his left hand in a single movement. With one final look around the camp, he gave a whistle. Lakon sprung up onto his feet, and the two walked to the open camp gates, heading for Tapae.

CHAPTER 3:
Forest Shadows

The four scouts had saddled their horses and quietly left the camp well before dawn. Lucius and his brother, Quintus, were accompanied by two other scouts, Appius and Flavius, all masters of their profession. Ruthless, cunning, and expert pathfinders, they were proud of their ability to merge into the background like ghosts. The four men dismounted from their horses; they had ridden as far as they dared under the cover of darkness.

As the sun rose, they tethered their horses at the side of the road to be collected by the vanguard. Now on foot, their mission was to reconnoitre the first ten miles of the road, looking for a suitable position for the overnight castra to be built. Ten miles, under normal circumstances, was only half of what a legion would cover. A legionnaire with a ninety-pound pack was trained to cover twenty miles. Under exceptional circumstances, they could do twenty-five miles and still be strong enough to engage an enemy.

Dacia was different! The road to Tapae was only fifty miles but made of narrow forest paths, no wider than two carts at best. On each side of the track grew thick, dark forests. Light barely penetrated through the canopies of the trees ranging a hundred feet above. The roads were unforgiving. Rutted, uneven, and growing ever steeper. Often, springs from unseen waterfalls high in the forest would be running across, eroding the soil towards the mountainside.

Quintus turned to Lucius and quietly said, "I can see there will be real problems." "The engineers will have to be out early to start clearing the way for the legions. Even so, they will have to reduce formation and make the best of whatever space they have." "The oxen and supply carts will be an even bigger issue."

Lucius nodded, followed by, "This is going to be a far greater challenge than Fuscus had counted on; it will really reduce the miles they can cover in a day. I know our orders are ten miles but we should also look at eight as a safeguard, too. We have only covered six miles ourselves in four hours, some on horseback."

The two other scouts, Appius and Flavius, had forged ahead and were now waiting at a sharp bend in the road. As Quintus and Lucius watched them, the two in front urgently waved their hands inward and disappeared into the edge of the forest. Quintus and Lucius immediately ducked into the undergrowth and slipped under the cover of a large bush.

As day broke at the stronghold, a large detachment of engineers and legionnaires had set out armed with pickaxes, axes, and tree hooks. Their orders were to clear the route as wide as possible, enabling the main force to travel upward as quickly as possible. Deep along the forest road, orders were being barked as legionaries swung their axes, hacking at the thick tree trunks. The sound of wood splintering echoed throughout the forest. Large flocks of birds squawked and burst from their roosts into the early morning sky. The noise, the dust, the shouting, there was no disguising the presence of the Roman war machine. Soldiers worked in pairs, one cutting, the other dragging away branches and smaller logs.

Where they found the ground was uneven, teams of legionnaires wielded mattocks and shovels, levelling wherever possible for the marching columns. As in the building of the stronghold, the assigned men knew what was expected of them, and progress was slowly but surely being made.

To defend the workers from surprise attack, velites and auxiliaries scanned the tree line for movement. Archers stood ready with arrows nocked, watching for the slightest indication of an attack. A rear guard, led by a centurion, kept watch for any flanking manoeuvres.

Cornelius Fuscus sat on his stallion, watching as the Vanguard eventually started to climb the initial incline up the winding path into the forest. The six-man wide, fourteen-deep formations of the first cohort were already having to adjust their positioning. The road, although enlarged by the engineers, required them to move inward, affecting their marching pace and rhythm. Marching packs (*sarcina*), cooking pots, clothing, and entrenching tools all hung from a *furca* (wooden pole) across their back. As the space narrowed, they were forced to tread carefully to avoid bumping into one another, occasionally spilling out toward the forest's edge.

The following cohort, now finally underway, was forced to reduce its pace to avoid colliding with the rear of the first. Fuscus reflected, only one thousand men were on the move. Thousands were still to follow along with carts, animals and cavalrymen. He knew if the road was too narrow for the column, even at only a few places, it would create major disruption. Those marching farther to the rear would be left waiting for hours. Exhausted and lacking discipline, they could fall out of formation. The foremost troops stretched out in much the same way, it would cause the entire column to break apart. Fuscus called out to the Praefectus Castrorum, "Ensure that suitable intervals are left between the cohorts; we must minimise any march blocks. Did you see? We're already having problems."

The Praefectus Castrorum knew it was critical to maintain movement and communication alongside the column. Space had to be available to allow officers and messengers to get past. He immediately rode over to the next cohort and gave the orders to delay. "Wait until I say proceed."

Fuscus, in his overall plan, had estimated there would be seventeen hours of daylight to move the column and build the overnight camp. Now, he knew it was going to be challenging. They would need every minute and a great deal of luck.

Titus and Lakon had slipped past the road crews early. Titus wanted to be away from the column and have the chance to think carefully about his orders.

By guile, by fire, by pain—make them tremble, make them weep. Discover their gold mines, the very veins that sustain their nation. Unearth the means to break them, he recalled the orders. He knew he had to get past Tapae and onward to their city, Sarmizegetusa Regia. He had to infiltrate and learn what he could. He needed to reconnoitre the city, find the weaknesses, and plot where he could create the most havoc.

As the road became steeper and more uneven, he decided that he would walk to rest his horse.

Lakon came bounding out of the forest just ahead of him, his head covered in fern and leaves. "At least someone is enjoying this," Titus said to Lakon

Titus dismounted; he tied his coat over the saddle horn, and the pair set off up the ever-steepening road.

Appius had seen a flash of colour in the distance and had pulled Flavius back into the undergrowth. With his other hand, he quietly warned the brothers further back down the trail. Appius thought he had seen them disappear into the undergrowth following his warning but couldn't be sure. They both waited in silence, keeping cover for what felt like an eternity.

Deciding that it would be safer, although slower, they made their way deeper into the fringes of the forest trying to keep as close to the tree line as possible. As they crept forward, with Appius leading, they heard a noise. Both men froze. It was a subtle, hushed crack as though a foot had gently stood on a dry branch. They waited and listened but nothing. Appius silently beckoned to Flavius, and the two men moved towards a large oak that offered cover, yet still gave them a clear view of the scene ahead.

Another crack made them drop to their knees, their eyes squinting through the undergrowth to see what made the noise. They heard it again; their hearts thumped in their chests as they struggled to control their breathing. Veins pumping, they quietly drew their daggers. Wrists taut and the bone handle of the blades held tightly in their grip, they prepared themselves to strike.

A badger lazily sauntered to within three feet of them, looked up, and twitched its nose. Then it scuttled off towards a fern-laden bank. Appius let out a quiet sigh of relief. Flavius looked at his hands; they were still shaking. He turned to Appius and muttered, 'A fucking badger."
Flavius laughed. 'It's lucky, it nearly lost its—

As he tried to get the last word out, the blade of a Dacian falx tore through the back of his head and burst from his open mouth. His head split in two as he dropped to the floor. Flavius looked on in disbelief and in utter shock. The Dacian warrior put his foot on Appius's back and pulled the falx out. In the same quick movement, he brought it down across Flavius's neck and shoulders, splitting him in half. In an instant and silently, they both were killed.

Zalmir stood looking at the two dead Romans. He and three other Dacian wolf warriors had been tracking them since dawn. Zalmir was a powerful man with broad shoulders and jet-black hair that merged with his enormous beard. He wore leather leggings and a dark brown tunic covered by thick leather breastplates. Over his shoulders, he wore a wolf's skin, with a snarling wolf's head covering a golden helmet. On the right-hand side of his belt, he had a three-foot curved bladed falx topped with a foot-long wooden handle. On his left side, a huge dagger with a golden handle was secured high on his waistband. Zalmir, if required, could wield these fearsome weapons simultaneously. Truly, he was a living nightmare, ready to strike fear into the hearts of the legions.

Thiamark, a warrior even larger than Zalmir, bent down and inspected the clothes of the dead men. He stood up, holding out the palm of his hand; it contained two wooden charms. "Nothing," he said quietly. "Just these worthless Roman gods, for what good they were to them."

The four men looked down and then spat on the bodies with contempt.

Zalmir stood still, gently sniffing the air. He raised his right arm and silently gestured to the three others. Two fingers were raised, and he pointed down the road towards where they had sighted the other two men.

They were agile for big men, moving through the forest silently and with ease. They had lived here all their lives; they knew every path, trail, tunnel, and stream. They could disappear and then rise up out of the undergrowth, seemingly as a phoenix would from the ashes. This was their land, and the Romans were going to pay dearly for daring to enter it.

Four miles down the road, the column was now making some progress. Although challenging, the road crews had steadfastly kept at their task, removing rocks, clearing undergrowth, and levelling the surface wherever possible. The Praefectus Castrorum had regularly rotated crews, maintaining a level of momentum with fresh men.

Morale was retained, and the workforce reinvigorated. Such was the challenge, inevitable injuries occurred. Hands were crushed, axes slipped, cutting into legs. Rotten trees were felled, large branches became airborne, striking unwary men with tremendous force and causing catastrophic wounds. The wounded were taken for treatment to makeshift medical tents that were pitched at various points on the road. The dead were left covered inside the undergrowth of the forest. Wooden markers showed where they could be recovered by the rearguard servants. Nothing was allowed to interrupt the column's steady march upwards towards Tapae.

Cornelius Fuscus rode in between the first and second cohorts, surrounded by a group of officers. He was feeling more optimistic; the Tapae road was being cleared, and they had started to put some miles behind them. He laughed to himself. Why did he always worry? The Roman machine was relentless ‑unstoppable. They were organised and disciplined, and no obstacle was too great to hold them back from their purpose. Domitian's orders will be fulfilled.

Fuscus kicked his horse, and it broke out into an instant canter, covering ground rapidly to link up with the first cohort.

Sextus could hear the horses' hoofs catching on the rough road surface. He thought to himself, *Fuscus, you are going to find yourself on the ground with half a tonne of horse on top of you if you don't rein in on this loose shit. I'm certainly not going to lift the thing off you.*

Fuscus reined in the horse roughly, bringing it to a slow walk, and then proceeded to walk alongside Sextus as he marched along. "Scouts," he shouted, "any communication back from them?"

Sextus shook his head, then said, "Nothing. We should have heard something. They were on the road well before dawn. Lucius is our most experienced scout; I have every confidence in him and his squad. They will report."

Fuscus considered the situation and then said, "If you don't hear back in an hour, we will send out another squad. Keep me informed."

Sextus saluted and marched onward with the first cohort.

Fuscus pulled the horse across to the side of the road and halted, allowing the rest of the cohort to pass by him. He sat back in his saddle, took a drink from his leather water bottle, and then rubbed the sweat off his face with the palm of his hand. He assessed the situation. It was just after midday, and they had been on the move for six hours. All five legions were making progress, although reduced to a marching formation of five abreast. He had made the decision to keep the majority of the baggage train and support units to the rear to avoid holding up the rear legions and reduce further rutting of the road surface. Five legions, almost twenty-five thousand legionnaires, creating a column two and a half miles long, all marched towards Tapae. The first was just reaching the fifth-mile mark. The road crews had performed their job superbly despite many casualties.

It was far from what Fuscus had planned, but they were in a better position than anticipated earlier in the morning. He took another drink from his water bottle and then spat out the road dust from his mouth. His mind went back to his last conversation with the centurion. *Where are those scouts?* he wondered.

They thought they could now hear the quietest of footsteps, moving through the undergrowth, far above them but moving fast. Drawing closer, they thought they could make out three or perhaps four sets of footsteps. Quintus looked at Lucius, put his finger to his lips, and signed for him to follow him. Quintus broke away from the large bush they were hiding under and drove deeper into the forest. His senses screamed as he tried to think what he could do to save them both.

The slightest of cracks came from high above them on the mountainside, but not enough to provide direction. It was as though they were floating above the surface of the forest. He couldn't hear birds being disturbed—*why?* They were like spectres in the shadows. His years of experience were flashing through his mind as he fought for their survival. He heard another noise, this time coming from in front of them but again too far away to see. He stopped and looked at Lucius, whose face mirrored exactly the fear he felt. They exchanged silent glances, and both pushed onwards, deeper into the forest.

Zalmir could hear them, scuttering through the forest as loud as deer. Birds exploded into flight from branches, giving him and his wolf warrior brothers clear signs of where and in what direction they were travelling. Zalmir laughed: "These pathetic Roman scouts could be caught by Dacian children!"

Quintus was running towards a tiny grass clearing when he saw it out of the corner of his eye. At first, he dismissed it, but on a second glance, he made his decision. He spun around to his right and headed off towards a grass bank. To the side of it was a small entrance to what appeared to be a hollow, large enough to fit the two brothers in. It looked as though it had been a badger set that had recently collapsed. Large ferns were growing over the top of most of it, with the floor sunken just enough to allow the men to lie flat out of vision.

In seconds, the brothers were in it. Quintus pulled his dagger free and quickly cut some large ferns that were within reach, covering the open front of their bolt hole.

Quintus whispered to Lucius, "Our backs are covered now. If we are going to die, those Dacian bastards are going to have to face us."

Lucius nodded and smiled.

Zalmir and Thiamark stopped running and signalled to the other two wolf warriors to wait where they were. They listened, but they heard nothing. No birds, no rustle from the undergrowth, or snapping of twigs. They stood still, listening to only the wind blowing gently through the trees and, in the far distance, Roman bastards carving through their sacred forest.

Thiamark turned to Zalmir and whispered, "They must have gone to ground. We would be able to pick them up otherwise, they stumble around like drunkards."

Zalmir replied, "Agreed. We will split up. You take Rhol and go downward on the northern side, and I will take Gen and take the southern side. We will pincer them."

The pairs of wolf warriors set off, as ever, seemingly floating over the forest floor.

For Quintus and Lucius, the waiting was agonising. Every noise, every movement, they expected the ferns to be ripped from their lair, followed by blades. As time went on, they thought they heard more footsteps, *but was it their minds playing tricks?* Quintus hoped that Appius and Flavius had kept clear of whoever was stalking them.

Thaimark and Rhol had made good ground; the forest on the northern side was slightly thinner. Every hundred yards, they stopped, listened and redirected themselves. Rhol, the younger of the two, pulled Thaimark's sleeve and pointed ahead of them but slightly south. At last, they could hear the Romans again. It was clear they were afraid, and had already begun making their way back towards the legions advancing from below. Thaimark smiled at Rhol and ran his finger across his throat. It was their turn for the kill!

The two wolf warriors set off, covering the ground in haste. They quickly came upon a small grass clearing, where the sunlight bathed thick ferns growing around a large grass mound. To the side was a large gnarly oak stump, which had fallen many years ago. The tree would have been enormous in its prime! They both stopped and listened. *Silence!* Then, they heard it again, and both gave out a wolf's howl.

Thaimark said, "The stupid Roman fools are running scared; they won't make it out alive. They will run straight into Zalmir and Gen's blades."

Quintus and Lucius sprang from their lair, daggers drawn. They covered the two paces between them and the unknowing wolf warriors in an instant. Grabbing them from behind, Quintus and Lucius covered their mouths and, with a single swipe, drew their blades across the throat of each man. Silently, they gently let them fall to the ground.

Without a moment's delay, Quintus said, "Quick-back into the lair."

The two brothers dived back into the hollow and carefully covered themselves with the ferns. Both men looked at each other, wild-eyed, shaking but still alive!

Zalmir and Gen had heard the noise, too. Although a distance away from them, it was clearly something large. They picked up their pace; the Romans were running scared and wouldn't be listening for other footsteps. Faster, they ran, covering ground in huge bounds. They were forest men from birth, balanced and nimble of foot. Gen was slightly smaller than Zalmir and, with less bulk, was in front of the pair, now running fast. He was young and wanted his first taste of Roman blood. All his childhood, he had heard stories around the campfires of Dacian wolf warrior's bravery. Now, he was one of them and wanted to prove himself.

The pair were close now. They could hear but still not see anything. There were two large oak trees in their way, standing four feet apart like guards to attention. Past the trees, there was a rough path that led from the Tapae road, leading inwards deeper into the forest. Gen took a giant leap to pass through the gap in the trees, aiming to land on the back of the path. He sailed through the air, passing the trees. With a flash of silver, a gladius struck him hard in the gut, ripping him open and sending him to the ground in a crumpled pile, screaming.

Zalmir was a yard behind and did all he could to stop himself careering through the gap, slamming hard against the left hand oak tree. He sprung to his feet, howling and tearing his falx free, ready to strike.

Titus stepped out from the back of the tree, his gladius covered in blood. Zalmir drove forward in rage, swinging the blade with all his force. Titus neatly took a step to the side, allowing the falx to swish past his shoulder, and it rebounded as it hit the tree. Titus lunged and clipped Zalmir's side but did not generate any real damage.

In a moment, the Dacian blade was coming through the air, Titus's used all his strength to parry the blow. Zalmir, in an instance, pulled out his long dagger and, with both arms wielding weapons, was now pushing Titus backwards to the large oak. Titus had nowhere to move. He tried to fend off the attack as best he could, defending against the falx. There was a flash of the dagger, and it bit into the top of his shoulder, piercing between his lorica segmentata. Zalmir smiled and readied to make the killer blow.

Like a blur, Lakon hurled himself out from behind the tree and struck Zalmir at full speed, knocking him flat to the ground. Zalmir's arms flew wide, splayed out on either side of him. Zalmir was reeling, stunned from the force of the hit. Titus dived and rammed his Gladi straight into Zalmir's heart, killing him instantly.

Titus rolled off the body and lay panting and shaking beside it. He slowly pulled himself to his feet, the blood trickling down from his cut shoulder. Lakon excitedly rubbed his head against his legs and then shook his mighty frame, with blood flying off in all directions. They looked at Zalmir, lying cloaked in his wolf's skin. Even in death, he was a fearsome sight.

They both heard the sharp snap, followed by a piercing howl coming from behind them. Lakon reacted first, instantly launching himself high and fast towards the young wolf warrior. Gen came staggering at them both, falx in hand and howling. In a single movement, Lakon hit him hard and ripped out his throat as they fell.

Titus looked down at Lakon, now sitting quietly next to the body of the young man. He thought, *Such a faithful companion, yet a killing machine.*

Titus and Lakon slowly made their way back along the narrow path. The noise of the Roman road crews grew steadily louder as they forged ahead towards Tapae. Lakon suddenly growled.

A shout came from within the forest, "Keep that fucking killer away."

Titus whistled, and Lakon instantly sat motionless and silent.

Quintus and Lucius sheepishly came out of the forest shadows. Smeared in blood and mud, they greeted Titus. "Where the fuck did you come from?"

Titus replied, "I was deep in the forest and saw the four Dacian warriors come down behind the other two scouts. They were butchered. Sadly, I couldn't get near enough to save them. I watched your kill. You were both smart to run into the glade and hide in the hollow. I think the other two wolf warriors were confused by Lakon pushing through the undergrowth, thinking it was you running."

The group reached the Tapae road just as the road crew turned the corner below them. Quintus and Lucius bid farewell and sprinted off down the hill to meet up with the main column and report.

Titus looked at Lakon, his battle-scarred face still covered in the young wolf's blood. He patted Lakon hard on the back and was greeted with a gentle growl. The morning had past and still, they had made no progress in their quest. Titus turned and looked up the steep, uninviting hill towards Tapae.

CHAPTER 4:

Dacian Demons

High in the swirling mists of the Carpathian Mountains, two men stood on a shallow ridge. Slowly, they each surveyed the scene below them.

One was a huge wolf warrior, whilst the other, an aged high priest. The warrior was dressed in a full wolf skin, with the beast's head as his crown. A thick black beard blended seamlessly with the fur of the wolf. His piercing brown eyes, created an illusion that the wolf was alive. A thick quilted jacket covered a toughened leather breastplate, further adding to his enormous bulk. On his right arm, a golden wolf-headed armlet, a gift from King Decebalus, was proudly displayed. He was the high commander of the Dacian wolf warriors, the most feared of the Dacian tribes.

Two long, curved falx swords hung from his belt, their razor-sharp edges glinting ominously. In his expert hands, they became instruments of precison.

Capable of hooking or splitting shields and severing any exposed limbs instantly.

The holy man was smaller in size and slender. A large eagle claw necklace, interlaced with golden feathers, hung loosely from his neck. A dark brown wolf head tattoo with huge fangs was spread across the whole of his bald head. Complemented by a wolf skin drapped over his shoulders. In his right hand, he held a large staff topped with a golden wolf's face, it's emerald green eyes glowing.

Alongside the men high on poles were two raised Draco standards. Dragon-headed in form, they had wolf-like jaws and forked tongues that stuck out from their mouths. Their bodies, made from fabric, filled as the wind passed through them, creating a high-pitched shrill, screaming like a tormented demon.

The high priest reviewed the scene below, then turned to the warrior with a broad smile on his face and said, "Tarbus, the Romans dare to come! We taught them a painful lesson in Moesia, and they foolishly believe they can strike here in our homelands. Bendis, our sacred goddess of the forest, hears our prayers and receives our sacrifices. The blood of the Roman fools will nourish the sacred forests! They will learn never to stand on Dacian soil."

Tarbus slowly turned to face Vezinas, his friend of many years. "Bendis did indeed receive our prayers," he said, " but we will need more than her continued compassion and protection to watch over us. Our forest goddess and her spirits will not hold them back. It will be our warriors, Dacian strength, and belief in our great leader, King Decebalus, that will free us of them. Our tribes throughout the Carpathian Basin, pose a major threat to Rome. We are galvanised, resilient, and an unstoppable force who will challenge Roman supremacy."

Tarbus thought back to the previous morning and smiled. He had seen a lone eagle riding the rising thermals. Circling and gliding, she fiercely scanned for an unwary prey. Tucking her wings tightly into her side, she effortlessly plunged into a steep dive, instantly becoming a blinding blur of speckled brown. She broke her dive mere inches from the ground, raptor-like talons outstretched, and snatched a mountain hare just as it emerged from its burrow. As it squealed and writhed, she snapped its spine and pinned it to the earth in one fluid motion. The eagle picked up its prey and soared up into the morning sky, seeking out its cliff-top eyrie and her hungry brood.

Tarbus had stood mesmerised by the scene he had witnessed. The speed, strike, and the instant dispatch. The eagle was a refined killer. He smiled, thinking how

Dacian warriors were the same as that eagle. Fearless, merciless, and deadly.

Since the arrival of the Romans on the far bank of the Danube two months previously, Tarbus had been preparing for their invasion. He and Decebalus had spent many hours studying the meticulous Roman preparations. They intensely watched the calculated efficiency of the engineering. As the floating bridge spanned the river, the Dacian chiefs began to understand the arrogance of the Roman plan. Carefully and skillfully, they formulated their own response.

On leaving Titius, the brothers, Quintus and Lucius, made their way back down the road towards the marching column. A squad of archers guarding the road crew saw them approaching. With practised ease, they nocked their arrows, ready to strike. Every step was measured and watched until they were certain of the approaching scouts. The road crews were purposely attacking the dense forest, sawing, hacking, and chopping through the undergrowth. Occasionally, a legionnaire would stop briefly, look at their blood and mud-stained tunics, and simply return to work.

Centurion Sextus Aemilius, marching at the head of the first cohort, caught sight of Quintus and Lucius just after the vanguard had passed six miles.

As they drew near, he shouted a stream of questions, "Where the fuck have you been? You're over three hours late in reporting. Praetorian Prefect Fuscus wants your blood. What's happened to the other two?"

Quintus took a quick look at Lucius and replied, "Wolf warriors, Appius and Flavius, are dead. Titus saw them butchered."

Lucius joined in and said, "He and that killer dog of his got two of them. We killed two others."

The centurion replied, "Did you see signs of others? What about the stronghold reconnoitre?"

Quintus's face flushed as he said, "We only got to half a mile above here before we were picked up by the wolf warriors."

Sextus laughed out loud. "The best that Rome can produce, and you two get picked up like a pair of babes in the woods. You should both be fucking ashamed of yourselves."

Quintus and Lucius fixed Sextus with burning stares, their bodies rigid with rage.

The sound of hoofs came thundering up the road, breaking the immediate tension. Cornelius Fuscus, along with three other officers, rode up to the group. Fuscus instantly shouted, "Centurion, report."

Sextus stood to attention and said, "These two have just crawled out the woods, scared by a bunch of puppies! They lost two of their own when they were running away."

Fuscus scowled at the two scouts, followed by, "Stronghold position?"

Sextus replied quickly: "Nothing to report. They wanted to save themselves instead of the column."

Fuscus turned to a tribune and said, "Detain them; send them to the back of the column. I will deal with them later."

Quintus and Lucius were immediately grabbed by four guards accompanying the tribune. Their hands were tied behind them, and they were dragged away, screaming and protesting their innocence.

The Praefectus Castrorum turned to Fuscus and said, "Prefect, what are our orders? Do we assign the road crew to clear the stronghold here, or do we move on?"

Fuscus looked up at the sky; it was still clear, with only a hint of cloud in the west. He quickly calculated there were still eight more hours of light left. They could gain another two or three miles of march before halting to build the stronghold. This would allow the rear of the column and baggage train to catch up. "We move on," declared Fuscus. "Let's make the most of the light. Order the road crew to cover another two miles, then break ground for the stronghold."

Decimus Valerius Lupus, the Praefectus Fabrum (chief engineer), was happily reviewing the results that his squads were delivering. Even in this extreme environment, they were managing to keep ahead of the marching column. It had been his responsibility to build the floating pontoon bridge. He had proudly received personal congratulations from Cornelius Fuscus on its success. Now, he had again proved his worth, driving a wedge through the forest up the Tapae road.

The legions, although not moving at their usual pace, were at last gaining some mileage. Yes, there had been deaths and casualties, but it was for the greater good of Rome. *Surely, once these Dacian heathens are defeated, Fuscus will reward me with an even greater promotion,* Decimus thought to himself. He was so immersed in his own personal glory that he didn't hear the Praefectus Castrorum coming up the hill behind him.

He jumped as he heard, "Decimus, report!"

The men had known each other for many years, yet he still stood to attention. Decimus cleared his throat and said, "Squads advancing well. This part of the forest isn't so dense, so we should continue to make good progress."

"Good," said the Praefectus Castrorum. "Your orders are to progress another two miles, then stop and clear ground for the stronghold. You will get more resources to clear and build once the main vanguard reaches you."

Decimus replied, "Of course, it will be done."

The Praefectus Castrorum smiled and said, "I know it will. You are a good leader, Decimus. We urgently need the safety of the stronghold in these wild lands." He quickly mounted his horse, roughly pulled its heads round to face downhill, kicked it, and cantered back towards the vanguard and Fuscus.

Titus had decided the safest route for Lakon and himself would be to get to high ground. He might just have a chance to avoid the wolf warriors long enough to try to find an alternative route to Tapae. He decided to retrace his steps north along the forest footpath, then pick his way up to high ground. Hopefully, he would then be able to find a road leading across towards Tapae and on towards Sarmizegetusa.

He and Lakon followed the trail, ever watchful for any sight or sound of wolf warriors. The twin trees came into sight where Zalmir and Gen had been killed. Titus could see the warrior's bodies had already been removed, and in their place, two golden wolf masks with sparkling green emerald eyes hung on either tree.

As the dappled sunlight gently cast through the branches, the eyes sparkled as though on fire.

Titus knew he was being watched from deep within the forest. It was only the threat of Lakon that had stopped him from being immediately attacked. He had gone too far from the road, too far from the column, and the safety it offered. Now, only the silence of the wild surrounded him. His only course was to get off the path, try and seek high ground, and find somewhere that he could hide or defend.

He was going to have to outsmart them if he was to stand any chance of survival. He had to become a shadow, slipping through the terrain, ravines, caves, anything that offered cover. He picked up his pace and then cut away sharply from the path, deeper into the forest. He discovered that by shifting side to side, he could ease through the thick undergrowth with greater control and barely a sound. He was stepping high, avoiding tripping on the roots, slowly parting the bushes with his hands and carefully releasing them back. Lakon sensed the need for stealth and quietly followed Titus.

He eventually came across a dry creek bed. It twisted and turned but importantly, he could see it was heading uphill. Dry and silent for now but would become a roaring torrent during the rains. He let himself smile; he, at last, felt as though he was making some progress and heading to higher ground.

Lakon's heckles went straight up on his neck, and he growled. Softly as trained, but enough for the pair of them to stop dead in their tracks.

Titus could now hear footsteps, faint but clearly human. He instantly looked around him; there were a number of trees, but not large enough to hide behind. The footsteps were coming closer up the creek bed and fast. Titus turned and sprinted up the creek as fast as he could, avoiding large roots that had fought their way through to the once-living water source. He was covering the ground quickly. His mind was racing—*how could he get out of the riverbed and escape?* Still, he could hear the footsteps, and now, they were gaining on him. Titius considered stopping to face his assailants whilst he had some strength. Then, he saw it. A sharp bend appeared a hundred yards ahead, half-swallowed by thickened undergrowth. Titus sprinted on taking the bend at full speed. As he rounded the bend, he gasped in astonishment. The forest ahead had been utterly stripped of trees. As far as he could see across the hillside and down its slopes, it was bare. Once again, he heard the footsteps close behind him. He looked around and saw that on the right-hand side of the slope, there was a pile of big logs stacked high. He dashed over, followed closely by Lakon. Quietly, they hid and listened.

The footsteps hit the top of the hill and stopped. Two people! He heard muffled voices. They would know he hadn't made enough distance between them to make it across the clearing. There was only one possible place he could hide. Titus resigned himself to the gods and prepared.

They were really good! When they attacked, Titus had hardly heard a sound from them. Two wolf warriors, seemingly floating across the ground, falx in hand, came heading in fast towards them from either end of the logs. Only Lakon was ready. He jumped to meet the nearest to him and caught his blade arm tight in his mouth, locking on with an almighty crunch. As Lakon hit the ground, he pulled down with all his weight, twisting the man to the ground and instantly breaking his arm. He continued to hold on to the broken arm, and with all his force, he pulled backwards, shaking and thrashing, ripping the shoulder from its socket. An almighty scream filled the air as the pain surged through the warrior's writhing body. Lakon released his bite and, with a bound, grabbed his opponent's exposed neck, snapping it with a single powerful bite.

In the meantime, Titus was having a harder time. The wolf was fast, powerful, and experienced. He wielded the falx effortlessly, pushing his opponent backwards against the logs. It was only Titius's quick feet that allowed him to roll out from under a huge swipe of the blade and gain space between them. Titus made a powerful jab with his gladius, but at the last minute, feinted to the left, slashing the warrior's side.

He was countered instantly by a huge blow that he only partially managed to hold off. The curved tip of the falx tore his cheek and chest plate. It was followed up by a headbutt, splitting Titus's nose. He could smell the stench of the warrior at such close quarters as he pressed to take advantage of the strike. The wolf followed it up with a vicious slash from the falx aimed again at his head. Titus, though dazed, leaned sharply backwards, feeling the blast of air left by the passing blade. The warrior swung again, this time bringing it down hard towards his quarry's shoulder. Titus managed to block the mighty blow with his gladius, with the falx glancing away and hitting a log, instantly splintering the wood.

Although off balance, he managed to grab a small branch lying on the log pile with his left hand. He brought it sharply across the side of the wolf's head, stunning him. Immediately, he followed up with a solid lunge from his blade straight into his gut. The wolf looked at him in disbelief, then instinctively raised his falx arm to strike. Titus struck down hard across the top of his shoulder, severing the arm. With a final strike, he slit his throat. The wolf gasped and gagged as life drained from his body. His piercing dark eyes stared into Titus's, then he slipped down onto his knees and crumpled forward onto the ground.

Titus fell against the log pile, exhausted. He could still see the blazing eyes staring back at him. He shook his head, slowly pulled himself up straight, and looked for Lakon. He found him sitting by the body of the other wolf warrior, calmly licking a small cut he had received in the struggle. He jumped up, gently pushed his huge blood-covered head into Titus's hand, and growled affectionately.

Titus caught a powerful whiff of garlic! He laughed out loud and said, "I told you your breath could kill."

He patted him hard, and the pair walked back up to the top of the hill to inspect the site.

The Praefectus Fabrum was pushing his road crew hard; he wanted to ensure that Fuscus was delighted with him. He could see it now—promotion and a better pension. The woman he was secretly keeping, even though it was forbidden by army policy, would be even more pleased with him. And the GOLD—*don't forget the Dacian gold*. He would be awarded an appropriate share of the spoils as all of the legions would once they had victory. The rumours were that the Dacians gold mines were huge and that the quality was of the highest grade.

He could almost hear his friends telling him, *"Decimus, you are such a wealthy man and with such a beautiful wife and home. You must have been one of the bravest and cleverest men in your Legion. We are honoured to be your friends."*

He briefly closed his eyes and saw himself in his white toga, surrounded by his adoring friends! He lingered in that world for a second or two more, then opened his eyes. Behind him, a legionnaire slumped onto a tree stump, armour creaking, breath ragged with exhaustion. Decimus screamed at the top of his voice, "Get up, you lazy bastard. I'll have you flogged unless you get to your feet and move."

The legionnaire got up, turned away, and silently mouthed, "Fuck you" as he walked over to another large stump that needed removing.

Decimus looked up the road and assessed their current position. They had covered almost a further mile since Praefectus Castrorum had given him Fuscus's orders. One more mile to go, then they would clear the area required to build the stronghold. He told himself, *Without you, the campaign would fail.*

Titus looked across the open space. All that remained were rows of tree stumps as far as he could see. *Why?*

Lakon gave a bark. Titus looked over to the slope of the hill, where he could see Lakon pushing his head into the ground. He ran over and saw that there were huge trails leading down the mountainside. Long gauges had been made in the mud, surrounded by a vast amount of hoofprints heading downwards.

The pair followed the trail, stopping every hundred yards to listen for any noises. Half a mile down, the dense forest returned. Titus could now see that channels had been cleared, running left and right. They quietly walked along the right-hand channel and saw that a downward offshoot had been cut into the forest. He looked along the main channel and could see further offshoots had also been cut. They started to take one of these tracks when they heard voices. They were in the distance - *but clearly Roman.*

It all became clear to Titus in an instant.

Fuscus and his officers were riding alongside the third legion, who were making good pace. They were three miles behind the vanguard but had the benefit of the road being trampled by thousands of feet before them. With no rain, it had levelled the surface, making it easier for them to march.

Fuscus turned to an officer and said, "At this rate, we will make the stronghold before dusk. The more manpower available to the Praefectus Fabrum, the quicker we will have a secure Castra and safety."

The young officer replied, "You are right, Prefect, but who in their right minds would attack five of the best Roman legions?"

Fuscus smiled and said, "Fools."

Tarbus had ridden down to a lower ridge, allowing him a perfect viewpoint to see right through the lower reaches of Tapae road. He could now see in the distance, a never-ending snake of red and gold. Dust clouds loomed above them, as flocks of birds deserted the safety of the forest trees, creating a patchwork of black. It was time!

Tarbus turned to a wolf warrior standing by a smouldering, smokeless fire and said, "Put on the wet straw."

The warrior instantly grabbed an armful of straw and laid it on the fire. He picked up his shield and, with powerful blasts down, fanned the fire into life. The flames below grew until they hit the wet straw. Instantly, a plume of white smoke curled upwards, thickening fast as the straw beneath caught fire, hissing and spitting. Tarbus looked at Vezinas, the high priest and said, "Now, we make them pay."

CHAPTER 5:
The Wolf Bites

The wolf warriors had been impatiently waiting for the signal. For weeks, they had been planning, preparing, and rehearsing every single element. Even the smallest boy had a part to play and was ready to defend his homeland. There had been hours of backbreaking toil, training, and continuous rehearsal of roles. The smallest detail was tested over and over again, ensuring that the plan would not fail.

They had watched hidden in the dense forest as the Roman column slowly made its way up the Tapae road. Their anger boiled as they watched the road crews hacking and chopping through their cherished forest, clearing a path wide enough for the column and its entourage to pass. As the crews slowly made their way uphill, some members wandered deeper into the forest to relieve themselves. Had they known how close they were to having their throats cut, it would no doubt have loosened their bowels.

Now that the time had come, the wolf warriors slowly raised their heads out of their sunken burrows and silently peered out across the forest floor. Each group of ten men had dug trenches, wide and deep enough to allow the men to be seated. Wooden roofs had been fashioned from branches and twigs stuffed with ferns. These could be slid across the mouth of the trenches, providing total camouflage.

Moskon, who commanded one hundred wolf warriors, slightly raised his roof and looked along the trenches, first to his left and then right. As it he looked along the lines, it seemed as though the very bowels of the earth were erupting. Men who had entered the holes well before dawn were quietly surfacing head-high like cockroaches swarming from piles of rotting bark. The only warriors free to move were the patrols tasked with killing the Roman scouts. They were under strict orders never to return.

Bithus, Moskon's deputy commander, quietly joined him. Both men proudly exchanged glances; the first part of the plan had worked. But they stank!

Bithus whispered, "It's the last time I spend twelve hours with ten men in a grave."

Moskon replied, I wouldn't be so sure. If we don't get it right today, you'll be back with them for good before nightfall. He smiled, showing his black teeth as they protruded from his mouth. Moskon took one final look and then slowly stood to his full height.

Along the line of trenches, leaders of each group of warriors were watching him intently, waiting for the signal to move. Moskon anxiously looked up through the thick foliage, waiting for the agreed smoke signal, to appear high in the sky. At last, he saw the white smoke drifting upward. He carefully withdrew his falx from his waistband and pointed it forward. The hordes started to climb out of their trenches. At varying points all along the Tapae road, their comrades were enacting the same manoeuvre. The next stage of the plan was the most critical!

Quietly, they walked slowly down the channels, three men side by side. The forest floor in the channels had been cleared of all debris to avoid any unnecessary noise. The anxiety amongst them steadily grew to fever pitch as they approached their next position. As if to remind them, they occasionally caught the faint sound of a Roman voice on the wind. It was barely recognisable, yet unmistakably Roman. As they neared their position, Moskon held his falx high in the air. As one man, they all stopped instantly. He made a three-finger sign. A group of men peeled out and carefully pulled back wooden lids, the same camouflage as they had used to cover the trenches. They jumped into large trenches and started to pass out weapons. Gleaming axes, sharpe enough so to cut a hair! Falx and daggers that would slice through a shield. Nothing had been left to chance.

To maintain silence when walking from the trenches, all the weapons and axes had been placed back to back, covered with cloth. In silence, each wolf collected his weapons and walked the final two hundred yards to the next position.

As they lined up, Moskon pointed to the right, and the men all fanned out alongside many prepared log stacks, carefully stacked ten high. Eight feet in length, each log had been completely stripped of branches, and stumps. Nothing that protruded had been missed. All had been tied back by a criss-cross rope system and secured to large trees behind them. In the front of the logs, huge poles had been hammered in to help retain the weight of the wood.

Moskon made a further hand signal and a large number of men walked silently around the log piles towards the road. The ground had again been cleared for thirty feet to reduce the noise as they walked forward. The Tapae road was near, and the Roman voices marching upward were now unmistakable

At the end of the space was a line of large trees running the length of the log piles. At their bases, low-notch cuts had been made facing downwards towards the road. Five-foot-long, double-handed saws were lodged into the trees, and had been partially cut through. This meticulous planning had been repeated at chosen sites along the length of the road.

Fuscus and his retinue were back riding alongside the second cohort. They were about two hundred and fifty yards behind the first cohort, being driven forward aggressively by Centurion Sextus Aemilius. As Primus Pilus, his cohort had always been the best and most prestigious. It now contained the most experienced and skilled soldiers, and it was the strongest unit within the legion. They always led from the front, pressurising the rest of the cohorts.

Fuscus was now getting concerned as the gap between the first and second was widening further, alarmingly stretching out the column. Fuscus pulled his reins and kicked on his horse, shouting as he rode off, "I must speak with Centurion Sextus Aemilius urgently."

The retinue of officers frantically grabbed their horses' reins and chased after Fuscus as fast as they could.

Decimus, the Praefectus Fabrum, saw the smoke rise slightly further up the valley. He was at the head of the road crew. They had five hundred yards still to clear before his gangs would stop and work on clearing the stronghold site. He was furious; he had given his teams strict instructions not to light fires. *If those lazy bastards have slipped off ahead and started cooking, they will be crucified,* he stormed under his breath. *I will not give Fuscus any reason to reprimand me.*

He called two legionnaires over and screamed at them, "Go up to that fire and get whoever is there and bring them back to me. If they resist, kill them."

The men dashed off, running up the hill towards the smoke.

Sextus was pushing his cohort hard. Over the last two months, although building the pontoon bridge, he thought they had become lazy. It was time to change that! The terrain for the first cohort, although some clearance had been undertaken, was still rough underfoot. Divots, roots, and stream gulleys running across the path made the march extremely tough. Sextus was determined to forge a large gap between the first and second cohorts.

They are going to feel this, he thought as he pushed the pace. He could hear his men blowing and cursing. Their packs became heavier with every mile, whilst with heads bent downwards, they pushed onward up the ever-increasing steep gradient.

Sextus was feeling his old wounds; he wasn't quite as young as he used to be. Yet, he was a veteran of many campaigns and made of steel. He would never show any form of weakness in front of his men.

Alongside Sextus in the middle of the front row, the *aquilifer* (standard bearer), covered in a full lion's skin and wearing a silver full-face mask, was matching pace, step for step. He was drenched with sweat and breathing deeply. Yet, the eagle standard stayed proudly raised on its signum.

Lucius and Quintus were each tied by their wrists to a long rope that was attached to the back of a supply cart. A pair of huge oxen was pulling the cart, bellowing under its weight as they steadily pulled up the hill. The brothers were being jerked and dragged as they stumbled along the road, their wrists now raw and bleeding. As guards walked alongside them, they continuously shouted their innocence. In turn, each guard took pleasure in hitting them with the end of their pilum, telling them to "*Shut the fuck up, you cowards.*"

Lucius stumbled from the most recent beating and pulled his head back quickly to gain his balance. From the corner of his eye, he saw a whisk of smoke trailing up into the sky. The smoke was brilliant white, as if damp straw or wet wood had been used. He caught Quintus's eye and mouthed, "*That's not right, we don't light fires on the march.*"

Titus and Lakon had just started to walk down one of the forest channels when he heard a faint cough. It wasn't a clear cough; it was heavily stifled, almost as though it was coming from underground. They both dropped to the floor and lay still, watching and listening.

Within minutes, a wolf's head slowly rose out from the ground only fifty yards away from him. As Titus looked on, branch covered lids were gently pushed back. Heads, possibly many hundreds, all started to appear above the forest floor. Slowly, the commander stood up straight. He turned his head to the west, looking up through the treeline. Titus raised himself as high as he dared, looking in the same direction, and caught a glimpse of smoke. The warrior raised his falx up above his head, and with this sign, men appeared climbing out of many trenches.

Titus pressed himself and Lakon as low to the ground as possible. He watched as a wave of totally disciplined men silently formed up in threes and carefully started to walk down the channels. The only sounds he could hear were of the marching legions below on the road. Talking, coughing, unaware of the danger in the forest. As he watched, the wolf warriors quickly filed down the channels and out of sight.

Titus's brain was racing. How could he warn the legions? How could he get past the wolves without being caught and killed?

Lakon shifted next to him. A crazy plan came into his mind. It might not stop them, but it could just buy time.

Moskon stood alongside Bithus and gave the order. Pairs of men moved swiftly forward towards the trees in front of them. Each pair of men grabbed the handles of the saws, looked straight at Moskon and waited. Bithus turned and walked behind the nearest piles of logs and stood with his hand outstretched. All along the lines of log piles, warriors stood with axes in hand, ready to strike!

Moskon nodded. Pairs of men started a slow rhythmic sawing, drawing the long, finally sharpened blades across each tree. With every cut, the blades sunk ever deeper into the trunks. Now aligned with the deep notches cut on the opposite side of the trunk, they were nearing completion. Moskon looked up at the trees; it wouldn't be long.

A whistle sounded high above the sound of the sawing. A shrill that grew louder and louder. Bithus turned and was faced by Lakon in full attack mode. Before he could react, the enormous dog slammed into him with tremendous force, hurling him hard against a pile of logs. He rebounded and fell head-first onto a large, crooked tree stump, instantly breaking his neck. Lakon didn't stop. He charged on, grabbing and ripping at warriors in his line of attack. A devil from hell, creating chaos and mayhem.

Titus had crept close to the end of the channel before signalling Lakon to attack. As the war dog leapt forward, Titus broke cover. He had estimated it was a hundred and fifty yards down to the road. He sprinted down towards the line of trees. Pairs of men sawed frantically as some of the trees began to sway and creak. Moskon saw the roman charging forward. Silence was no longer the order of the day, as he screamed at the top of his voice, "Stop that man." Three warriors heard the shout, and ran at full speed towards Titus as he cleared the tree line.

The two men were scrambling up the steep gradient, falx in hand, raised to strike. Titus, gladius in hand, met the first warrior at full speed, striking first. He drove his blade straight into the leading man's face, twisted, and withdrew it in one lethal motion. The second wolf heard the screaming and hesitated for a split second. Titus threw himself at him, arm locked straight, using the blade as a spear. He hit him square in the chest, releasing the handle as the gladius sunk up to the hilt.

Titus, weaponless, kept running. He could hear the third wolf howling and charging down after him. He couldn't look back. He was shouting "Ambush!" at the top of his voice, with no concern for how close the wolf was to him. He had to keep running, had to make the road. The legions were now barely fifty yards in front of him. He knew the man was almost on him. He could hear every step of the legions and the cursing of the wolf closing in. His senses were exploding. His lungs were bursting. He was almost spent. The wolf was upon him now, and he heard the blade swish through the air. Too late...

He felt the full weight of the wolf as he slammed into him and braced himself for the approaching final darkness. He was thrown to the ground, his momentum sending him sprawling head-first onto the road. Titus opened his eyes. All around him were legionaries' dirty, bleeding feet and their stinking, studded sandals. Behind lay the body of the wolf, a legionnaire pilum sticking through his neck.

Lakon continued to run, the screaming and shouting slowly getting quieter behind him. He had created havoc amongst the axemen. Before they could gather their senses and defend themselves, he had disappeared back into the dense forest. A telltale trail of blood and death was the only lasting sign of his visit.

Moskon screamed at the men, sawing wildly, "Finish it. Finish it!"

As his words echoed through the forest, a huge tree wobbled, slowly tipped, and then fell straight towards the legions on the road. Tree after tree followed suit along the line. All long the Tapae road, trees continued to fall.

Sprinting back behind the logs, Moskon saw Bithus. His neck, at right angles, was stuck in the stump, and his body strewn across the path.

Moskon roared, "Remove the poles. Cut the ropes. They have to be released now!"

The warriors hammered away at the supporting poles retaining the piles of logs, weakening their hold. In an instant, the axemen cut the ropes, and the logs broke frec. Moskon shrieked, "Die, you Roman bastards!"

Sextus heard the almighty roar as the tons of logs careered down the slope. As they gained speed, they bounced and spun, ricocheting off each other, boiling like a cauldron of death. They struck the felled trees, many spun and twisted upwards, while others picked up speed, bumping and bouncing down the length of the trunks. Whichever route they took, all headed downwards into the path of the stricken legions.

Over the roar of the tsunami of logs, Sextus screamed at the top of his voice, "Save yourselves!"

Sextus spotted a huge rock by the roadside, twenty yards ahead to his left. He could hear the logs growing ever closer, cracking and splintering. He had just one chance to save himself. He sprinted with all his might and dived headlong as the first of the logs came whistling over him at shoulder height. He pulled himself tightly into a ball and sheltered behind the rock.

All along the road, the legionnaires were caught square on to the blast. The logs had become a boiling avalanche, instantly tearing great swathes of men from the road and hurling them over the mountainside to their deaths. The logs that struck obstacles on their way down had splintered into massive shards. They flew through the air like great spears, impaling and mangling the bodies of the legionnaires still remaining on the road. Many of those not killed instantly now lay writhing and screaming in agony.

Titus was screaming, "Ambush! Ambush!" as loud as he could. The legionnaires looked at him as though he was mad.

As he scrambled to his feet, he heard the sound. A legionary who had stepped forward to inspect the warrior was struck full in the chest by a massive flying splinter. The force of it threw the man in the air and swept both Titus and himself across the road, over the verge and down the mountainside.

Fuscus and his retinue were galloping between the first and second cohorts when the trees came down. The five of them were now alone in a gap, separated from both cohorts by huge trees across the road. Fuscus wheeled around and around on his horse as he witnessed firsthand the horror of the attack. Many hundreds of his men on either side of him were being slaughtered. He 'screamed out' in horror. But there was nothing he could do!

Further back in the column, brothers Lucius and Quintus were being dragged along when suddenly the cart stopped. They both fell to the ground as the tension on the rope was released. They could hear shouting coming from further up the road and see huge clouds of belching dust in the air. They shouted to the guards, "It has to be an ambush! Did you not see the smoke?!"

The nearest guard swung his pilum, knocking Quintus to the floor. "I told you to shut up."

Tarbus sat on his white stallion, looking down towards the valley. He had watched almost in slow motion as his plan had unfolded. The red and gold snake slowly advancing upward. The relentless tramp of their marching feet echoed through the mountains and forests like a waterfall crashing over rocks. The creaking and screeching of the trees as they were felled and tumbled headlong onto the road. The immediate isolation of thousands of men as they were corralled by the fallen trees. He saw the onslaught of logs as they spiralled downwards, their deadly trajectory plotted and unswerving. The slaughter that followed was righteous.

The sound of the waterfall had vanished, replaced by the noise of living hell. Piercing screams echoed through the mountains, rising to an endless crescendo and then, abruptly, all fell silent. A chasm of eerie silence spread across the valley.

Tarbus looked at Vezinas. The wolf tattoo on Vezinas's head shone in the late afternoon light. He had a broad smile on his face. Tarbus let out a huge howl of satisfaction and relief. Turning to a wolf warrior standing nearby, he said, "Release them"

The wolf warrior walked across to a long, bronze war carnyx (horn), standing over six feet tall. It had a dragon's head with two tongues extending from its mouth. He picked it up and held it vertically. He took a huge breath and placed his lips on the central mouthpiece. Slowly, he released a controlled stream of air, allowing it to travel throughout the carnyx, eventually reaching the top of the instrument. A deep, haunting, and otherworldly wail proceeded to fill the air, piercing and terrifying as some bygone beast. He finished the first blast and repeated it, but this time with a longer blast.

It was immediately replied to by a host of howls reverberating around the whole mountain. The wolf warriors were ready!

CHAPTER 6:
Call of the Carnyx

Sextus's instinct for survival immediately engaged. Forged from years of battle experience, he quickly assessed his situation. He was uninjured, he had weapons, and he was, for the moment, in a safe place hidden behind the rock.

He laid flat and, very carefully, peered around the rock. Before him lay a scene of total devastation. Logs and trees were strewn throughout, resembling the chaos spawned by a fractured dam. Broken and mangled bodies lay crushed and trapped amongst the debris. Some had been speared completely through by splinters of wood the size of pilums. Their bodies hung suspended in the air as on the spindle of a child's spinning top. Sextus's years of war offered no preparation for this sight. His reaction was of utter repulsion. He broke out into an uncontrollable sweat, drenching him in seconds. A sudden desire to run built like a raging torrent. He started shaking uncontrollably and fought with all his might to stop himself screaming.

Then a sound. At first, he thought he was going mad. He heard it again. A voice. A Roman voice—no, Roman voices! Sextus knelt up and sought out the direction of the voices. He couldn't see who it was because of a large tree strewn across the road. The tree was balanced on top of a small rock, angling it slightly, leaving a foot of clearance from the road. Sextus moved postion and could then clearly see legionnaires' legs. Many legs. The fear subsided and was replaced by guilt and shame. He, Centurion Sextus Aemilius, Primus Pilus, had been reduced to a gibbering fool.

How could he ever live with himself? He heard the voices again. It slowly penetrated his brain, triggering a response from deep inside. He jumped to his feet and strode out from the rock, completely unconcerned for his own safety. His brain was racing: perhaps the situation wasn't as dire as it seemed. Could there be more groups alive throughout the rest of the column? He had to get to his men. His route to the tree was eighty yards of mayhem. Logs at every angle blocked part of the way. Piles of legionnaires' interlocked bodies created barriers as if direct from Hades. It was as if the king of the underworld himself had personally woven them amongst the logs. Sextus pressed on, blinkered like a warhorse, eyes locked on a single target. As he ran, the legionaries, their vision obscured on the other side of the tree, heard footsteps and shouted, "Who goes there?!'"

Sextus sarcastically replied: "Who the fuck do you think it is, you morons?"

A mighty cheer rose from the other side. Two burly legionnaires held up by their colleagues, reached over the large tree's trunk and pulled Sextus clear over to the other side. Sextus dropped to his feet and immediately took stock.

Fuscus and his five officers were alone, totally isolated from the first and second cohorts. They had heard the noise of the trees falling. The logs crashing down, the screaming and wailing of so many men as they were so easily slaughtered. The sound of the carnyx resounded all around the valley, followed by the blood-chilling wolf howl.

Fuscus looked at the eyes of his officers as they struggled to take in the situation. Although experienced soldiers, they had never been in a situation as terrible as this and looked to Fuscus for leadership. He looked at the Praefectus Castrorum, his most senior officer. Was he wrong, or did he detect a look of sheer disgust in his eyes towards him?

Fuscus asked himself, *Had I not done enough? Could I have prepared better? Did I push too far, too soon - without* waiting for the scouts to return? Did the lure of gold cloud my judgement? How could I, Cornelius Fuscus, Praetorian Prefect, have been so wrong?

A decade slipped away in Fuscus's mind. He had been a hero then. The memory shone as brightly as ever.

At first they were all in awe of the plume of ash and smoke that was spewing from the volcano's peak. Growing in size and steadily gaining height thousands of feet above. Lightning flashes started to appear as the atmospheric pressure started to change. Higher and higher, darker and darker, the cloud and smoke grew. Tremours started to rock the streets.

As the flakes of pumice started to fall, Fuscus gathered his family together - his wife and son, elderly father, along with his sister and her two children. He had told them all that they had to leave instantly.

His father shook his head and disagreed, "This house has been in our family for generations. It was built by Roman craftsmen of stone, has solid oak beams and the finest clay tiles for the roof. It can stand an earthquake. A few small stones will not chase me from my home."

Fuscus angrily walked over to the double doors that looked out to the veranda. A long sweeping garden led down towards the bay. The house possessed the most stunning view out towards the Mediterranean. In the distance, the Isola d'Ischia was shimmering, guarding the bay of Naples as always. Yet, something wasn't right. It took Fuscus a number of minutes to fathom it. Then he understood. It was the sea! Even in the time that he had been looking at it, the flat, calm surface was becoming a milky pond. It wasn't the sun's reflection. He could see small boats leaving a shimmering scum trail as they sailed through it. At that moment, a tremendous roar erupted from within Vesuvius.

Fuscus immediately ran to the stables and shouted at the servants, "Prepare the cart straight away and bring it to the side of the house!" He knew his next move had to be carefully accomplished and calmly walked back inside the house. By now, the family on hearing the earth shattering roar was becoming far more concerned, but his father was still remained resolute.

Fuscus's wife was standing at the back window, looking up at the volcano as it belched out huge quantities of ash and rock. It was now soaring thousands of feet into the sky. He whispered to her, "We all need to leave now. Gather my sister and all the children and go to the side door. You have to be calm and show no fear."

His wife looked at him with tear-filled eyes, nodded silently, and walked quickly out towards the rest of the family. Fuscus heard the cart approaching. There was only one thing to do. He saw a large tapestry hanging on the wall. He grabbed it and a sash that was hanging from it. His father had moved to the verandah and was now looking out to sea. Fuscus crept up behind him. The tapestry swept fully over his father's head and body, and, as gently as he could, he brought him to the ground. With military precision, he tied the sash around his father's legs and arms. His fathers screams and curses, filled the air as he hoisted his light frame up onto his shoulders and ran to the door, shouting, " Everyone, get on the cart now!"

Fuscus grabbed the reins and whipped onward the agitated horses. They took off with a jolt, and the family headed out towards the east gate. All around them, the streets of Pompeii were being covered with an increasing cover of pumice. It resembled a frozen January day. He expected to see children out playing and laughing in the snow. His father's curses snapped his thoughts back, and he whipped the horses hard, driving them onward, sweat flying and foam gathering at their bits.

Common sense would be to head west towards the sea and away from Vesuvius. Was it the crowds of people heading west or some divine intervention that made Fuscus drive east? He would never know. As the cart passed wide behind the base of Vesuvius, there was an almighty explosion. A huge pyroclastic flow spewed forth, speeding down the volcano. Firstly, racing towards and obliterating Herculaneum before changing direction and completely engulfing Pompeii. The city and its whole western seaboard were submerged under yards of ash and pumice, killing thousands of people.

The sound of the Praefectus Castrorum's voice shouting, "I can hear voices," jolted Fuscus back from his thoughts. He continued, "It's coming from ahead. It must be the first cohort."

As Fuscus looked towards the fallen tree, he could clearly make out the outline of legionnaires starting to climb over towards them. A junior officer had already galloped across and screamed out, "Report!"

The gravelly voice of Sextus shouted, "Three hundred of the first cohort have survived, many wounded but still able to fight!"

The junior officer just mouthed silently, "Five hundred gone. The Gods help us."

Lucius and Quintus, although still tied to part of the cart, had survived the logs. Their guards had rushed forward to see what had caused the column to stop and were instantly caught in the maelstrom. All four were driven, tumbling across the road straight into the rocky valley below. The brothers owed their survival to the four massive oxen hitched to the cart. The logs that slammed into the beasts were deflected, crashing instead into the heavily laden wagon. Miraculously, though the cart splintered into pieces, the logs soared over Lucius and Quintus as they lay pressed into a rugged trough in the road.

When the noise subsided, Lucius was the first to look up. Cautiously, he got to his knees and wiped the sweat from his brow, all the time listening for any sound of footsteps. Quintus, his face splattered in oxen dung, joined Lucius, and together, they gazed upon the horror that unfolded in front of them. Lucius knew they had to act. They had to get free of the rope. He jumped to his feet and started looking around for a blade. Behind the smashed bodies of the oxen, he could see a group of legionnaires lying in a grotesque bundle. He shouted at Quintus, "Get up, help me!"

Quintus stumbled to his feet, still in shock, as Lucius rushed to the end of the rope. It was still knotted to a smashed part of the cart, and they remained prisoners. The pair grappled with the fractured side of the cart and finally lifted it. Stumbling and tripping amongst the strewn wreckage, they made their way across to the legionnaires. Lucius spotted a gladius lying unsheathed on the road. Gripping the top of the blade in his right hand, he drew its edge carefully across the rope. With a sawing motion, he sliced through it and freed his wrists. Lucius swiftly spun the gladius and seized its handle. Quintus thrust out his hands, and within moments, they were both free.

As they rummaged through the dead legionnaires' bodies, Lucius softly said, "These poor bastards won't need these anymore."

They armed themselves, snatched up water flasks, and gathered whatever scraps of food they could find. Lucius grabbed hold of Quintus, his face grave, and said: "We have to move; the wolf warriors will be coming."

Tarbus jumped off his horse and ran over to Moskon. They exchanged a firm salute, crossing their arms over their chests in a gesture of respect.

Moskon spoke hesitantly, "Father, Bithus was killed. A Roman devil dog." Moskon pointed behind them and led Tarbus across the clearing and back towards the gnarled stump.

Bithus's body had been laid out in tribute, draped with his wolf skin. Tarbus looked down at his younger son, then bent and gently pulled the skin from his face. He carefully lifted his eyelids, gazed into the now clouded black eyes, and whispered so softly that even Moskon could not hear. Tarbus stood up, reached out, and held Moskon's shoulders tightly. Looking him straight in the eyes, he warmly smiled, saying: "Bithus's soul is now immortal. He will run with the wolves forever. You and I will run with him, too, when our names are called."

Moskon's nodded as his eyes filled, and then he sharply turned away.

Vezinas, the high priest, carefully replaced the wolf skin over Bithus' face. He gently touched the warrior's head whilst voicing an ancient chant. His words appeared to hover around the warrior's body and then, on release, float upward into the forest canopy.

Tarbus turned to Moskon and said, "Now is the time." Moskon nodded and replied, "Father, we are ready."

Titus had heard the scream, then felt the full force of the legionnaire hitting him. He instantly was travelling through the air in slow motion, arms and legs flailing as he flew across the road. The legionary, still screaming, tumbled past him and spiralled downward, vanishing out of earshot.. Titus fell towards a thick hawthorn bush growing a few feet from the edge. He reached out, thorns ripping deeply into his hands. The bush started to snag the arms of his tunic, tugging and gripping, slowing him down. Grinding down through the bush, his momentum was stalled, and he ground to a halt just inches from the sheer drop.

Fifty feet below him, the broken bodies of thousands of legionnaires were strewn across the valley floor. As he lay head first over the edge, he saw the occasional arm or leg twitch or heard a sudden piercing scream resonate upward from the valley.

Fuscus walked over to Sextus and softly said, "Centurion, you and I have served together for many years. We have fought our way out of a number of tight situations. I could always rely on you to fight through with the First. We have three hundred from the First Cohort, and only two hundred from the Second who have it across to us. Five hundred men against a nation of wolf warriors. Our honour must be in protecting the standard."

Sextus looked across towards a group of legionnaires who were standing, surrounding the eagle. In the midst of them, covered in blood, stood the aquilifer. His silver mask had long been lost when he was pulled out from under a pile of bodies. Broken but not beaten. In his battered hand, he still held the signum, swaying slightly, but the eagle was still erect, proudly on display. Sextus replied, "I will gather the remaining men."

Fuscus nodded and said, "We fight for Rome and our standards honour."

Decimus the Praefectus Fabrum was checking the placement of the stronghold when he heard the rumbling noise of the logs. It was quickly followed by screams and shouts that reverberated up the valley to him. His men instantly dropped their tools and started out of the forest down towards Decimus. As they gathered around him, the blast from the carnyx echoed across the valley, answered by the chilling wolf warrior howls!

Decimus shouted, "Does anyone know what has happened or seen anything?" As he finished his sentence, a young water boy ran up the road, tears streaming and in hysterics.

He could hardly get his words out, bumbling, "They're all dead. Logs exploded out of the woods and drove them all over the edge." The boy started screaming again. Decimus grabbed him, shook him, and slapped him hard around the face. The boy, shocked by the blow, still in floods of tears, abruptly stopped screaming.

Decimus was a big man and towered over the boy. He squatted down onto his knees and softly asked, "Are they all gone? Did you see anyone alive?"

The boy caught his breath and, between sobs, answered, "I don't know how many. I did see the Primus Pilus sheltering behind a rock, and I thought I could hear others."

Decimus gently tapped the boy's shoulder and thanked him for the report. He stood up and said, "There are five hundred of us, including fifty archers; we have to help those who have survived. Gather your weapons and form up."

Sextus called the remaining centurions to him. There were only left. These were battle-hardened men with years of experience. He didn't have to explain their situation; they knew the challenge. Sextus asked, "What is our status on weapons?"

The legionnaires hadn't wasted time. They had collected every usable weapon they could find from the bodies. The report came back quickly: "Every man has a Gladius and their Pugio dagger. There are three hundred scutums and four hundred pilums."

Sextus frowned and growled at them, "We are going to have to make each and every one of them count."

Fuscus walked over to the group and called them all to attention, "Legionnaires, when they attack, it will be fast and from the forest. We have a sheer drop behind us providing safety, so we need to cover our flanks. On the Primus Pilus command, those of you with a scutum will form a testudo (tortoise), giving protection from projectiles. Those without form at the rear with the pilum and make each one pay. Once they have all been used, be prepared to reinforce any of your fallen colleagues."

Tarbus gave the command. The carnyx called again, and the wolf warriors replied. All along the Tapae road, thousands of warriors howled. The sound of their running and howling could be heard rushing from the depths of the forest. This time, it wasn't a secret attack. They had the numbers and the tactical advantage; it was time to finish Domitian's legion swine completely. As they reached the edge of the clearing, their drawn falx blades caught the late afternoon sun, as streaks of light danced up into the canopy above.

Sextus had paced out a hundred-yard marker from their chosen defensive position. As the warriors reached it, Sextus barked out, "Testudo!"

The legionnaires, who had been drilled mercilessly all their careers, instantly engaged. As the wolf warriors charged forward, three hundred men effortlessly and calmly assembled. Thirty ranks wide and ten ranks deep, they created a hundred feet long perfectly formed red-shelled scutum testudo. They were the 'best of the best' and in the first cohort for good reason.

Fuscus was standing at the rear with the other officers, gladius drawn. He had one eye watching the testudo as it formed and interlocked whilst he automatically judged the distance of the rapidly approaching wolf warriors. "Wait for it, ten more feet," Fuscus said to himself. In an instant, he barked out a sharp order, "Pilum lose, make them count."

The air was filled with wooden-shafted javelins, each five feet long. Their iron tips were fitted with shanks, creating perfectly balanced weapons designed for maximum impact. The shank had been designed to lodge and bend on impact. If it hit a shield, it would penetrate and latch in. The quarry then had no choice but to discard it and was exposed to the gladius.

The sky above the testudo darkened as the first flight of pilum streaked above. They arched, then swooped down, striking the charging wolf warriors. As the pilum hit their mark, a hundred warriors were stopped dead in their tracks. The force of the impact knocked many of them backwards into the path of the warriors behind, creating a tumbling, hollering, and bloody mass.

Fuscus calmly ordered, "Prepare the second flight. Wait for my command."

Sextus, in front of the testudo, spoke to his men. "Hold your line. Remain silent."

As the shock wave of the first flight of pilum registered, the air erupted with screams. Initially, just a few, but quickly building to a crescendo, the searing pain and shock registered within the front-line wolf warriors. Again, the valley reverberated with the sound of pandemonium and torment.

Still, they came. Wave after wave, pressing down through the forest. Some stopped and pulled the dead and dying away. Others nimbly leapt over and continued to charge, falx in hand.

Fuscus ordered, "Second flight release." The legionnaires heaved back and then pulled the pilum through, their shoulders burning as they threw with all their might. Again, the pilum shot across the sky, streaking forward. Like angels of death, they glided silently through the air, finding their inevitable marks.

Sextus had taken up his usual Primus Pilus position. He stood outside of the testudo, scutum in hand. As commander, he had to see the battlefield clearly, assess threats, and give orders to adjust the formation as required. As the wolf warrior's spears flew in, he could see the testudo was holding well. Years of practice had made the interlocked testudo strategy almost impregnable to airborne attacks. Occasionally, an inbound spear might penetrate, but the disciplined legionnaires would close the gap from their fallen colleagues seamlessly. Sextus's practised eye automatically tracked the inbound spears aimed towards him, holding up his scutum just at the right moment to intercept them.

He had counted the waves of the pilum. He said to himself, "One more complete flight and then possibly a few stragglers, then we are exposed." He barked out to his men "Ready your fucking selves!" as the anger steadily grew inside him.

The piles of dead grew as the pilum hit their mark. Moskon had done his own calculations. Although he hated the waste of life, he knew that the Romans would be running out of pilum soon, plagued as they were by the masses of frontline warriors. He remembered Tarbus's words and smiled. *They will run with the Wolves forever.* He called to the wolf officers, "Prepare to hit the flanks. Pressure them. We have to break the formation!"

Fuscus turned to the Praefectus Castrorum. "This is it. The last few pilums. Now we shall feel the true force of the enemy."

He then shouted, "Release!"

The last flight soared out, a feeble shadow of the previous deadly storm. He looked over the battlefield, assessing the situation. Ahead, the testudo remained solid, a testimony to Roman warcraft. To his left, the aquilifer, unarmed, defiantly stood holding the eagle aloft. He was constantly calling out encouragement and warnings, supporting the cohort and keeping their spirits raised. Fuscus looked at the two hundred men in reserve. "Not enough!" he shouted. The Praefectus Castrorum nodded and looked towards Sextus.

A few wolf warriors had made it through to the testudo, avoiding the showers of pilum. As they swung their falx towards the interlocked scutum, a gladius would thrust straight out and penetrate the warrior's body. A simple kick and the blade would release and be retracted. Sextus looked at the bodies lying along the length of the testudo. "Not a fucking enough," he growled.

As he looked back to the forest, a full wolf wave, no longer hindered by pilum, was charging across towards him. Howling, screeching, rapidly covering the ground, whilst a flight of their own spears sped overhead towards the Romans.

Sextus tucked behind his scutum and screamed, "IN HOSTEM! Against the enemy!"

CHAPTER 7:
Time of Reckoning

Moskon was at the front of the wave, twin falx in hand, urging them forward. They were now almost forty yards away from the testudo. The flights of spears had been halted to avoid piercing their advancing warriors. Tarbus was standing at the edge of the clearing, studying the rigid Roman formation. He watched intently, constantly alert to any sign of sudden change in strategy. He had to get it right. Decebalus had personally entrusted him. They had meticulously worked together on the plan, reviewing and refining it. He was responsible for its completion. He had promised success.

Sextus, out of habit, shouted, "Keep the formation tight!" He chuckled. "Of course, it would be fucking tight. It's the first. When have they ever let me down?"

It was almost as if he needed to replay his own 'mantra' to appease the battle gods. He had lost count of the conflicts he had faced and won with these men.

Fighting their way through thick knee-deep mud, traipsing under full packs through scorching deserts with barely any water. They gave their all under any circumstance. One united band of brothers, proudly honouring their eagle standard and Rome.

Sextus gasped as he remembered how many had fallen in the ambush. He recalled his reaction to seeing the devastation of his cohort. Again, he felt the shame shiver run through his back and down into the pit of his stomach. How could he live with himself?

The front line of warriors was now just thirty-five yards from the testudo. A savage throng of wolf skins, howls, and jangling falx blades. Though hungry for battle, they remained disciplined, still completely under Moskon's command.

Sextus reacted to the sound of the hordes. He knew what was expected of him by his men. He was Primus Pilus. As the head of the elite cohort, he stood at the front with them. He would be engaged at the head of the fighting. Pushing back or driving forward, never seeming to tire. They all knew his voice. It changed at different stages of the battle, cajoling and cursing, "Mind your flank. Keep tight. Fucking kill that man!"

He was a man from the lowest rank who had risen right to the top by courage and skill. They all feared and respected him in equal amounts.

Sextus was ready. Gladius in hand, he stood up to his full height. His galea, topped with a bright red crest made of horsehair, made him tower above all in the cohort. He was a target for all to see and proud of his position. Scutum raised, he braced himself and waited for the full impact - just as he had so many times before. But it never came!

At thirty yards, a blast from the carnyx rang out, and the warriors stopped dead in their tracks. As they raised their falxes high, a howl of a thousand men penetrated the air. Above, a frantic burst of wings erupted high in the trees as nesting birds, startled in the early evening, shrieked in fury and scattered skyward.

At Moskon's command, two groups stepped out of the hordes, and walked forward to face the testudo. Maintaining a safe distance from the Romans, they slowly walked along the whole length of the formation, gesturing and taunting as they went. Amidst the uproar, Moskon's officers within the group carefully inspected the testudo. They reached the end of the front line and carried on walking around the flanks, reviewing, counting, and inspecting. Ever wary, they watched for rogue attacks breaking out from Fuscus's rear guard.

Fuscus stood open-mouthed. His anger boiling up inside him and ready to explode. He angrily spurted out to the Praefectus Castrorum, "Those bloody heathens are taunting us. They are actually fucking taunting us. How dare they fucking insult Domitian's army?!"

The Praefectus Castrorum turned to him, amazed by Fuscus's language, and said, "Not just taunting. Counting and inspecting, too. They know our weaknesses. Clearly, they have been planning their attack since we arrived. They are a force to be reckoned with."

On Moskon's command, slowly and deliberately, they walked back. Still taunting but now laughing and spitting at the group as they returned to the main body of warriors. The carnyx rang out again. The warriors, in a final act of defiance and antagonism, all urinated towards the Romans. They turned their backs on the testudo and walked back. As they did, a huge roar of laughter came from within the Roman ranks.

Sextus called to the cohort, "I am proud of you all. Fucking remember these insults; their time will come. Now be prepared."

The carnyx sounded again. This time, a long blast. Tarbus held up his falx, and there was total silence. "Now is the time," he said. "The Roman scum have dared to tread on Dacian soil. We must now cleanse their footsteps with their own blood."

Vezinas, the high priest, walked up beside Tarbus holding the Draco. As the Draco sang its shrill song,

Vezinas let out an almighty howl, whipping the warriors into a wild frenzy.

The carnyx blew again. Wave after wave of Dacian wolf warriors charged out across the clearing. Their eyes fixed on the testudo; ever closer, they ran to their target. Howling and screeching at the tops of their voices, they could see the eyes of the legionnaires peering through the small gaps of the scutum walls. Wild Roman eyes, whites exposed and pupils dilated, taking in every detail as the terror approached them. Straining and interlocking, they maintained formation. Years of relentless training and iron discipline holding fast, battling the primal urge to drop the shield and flee!

Sextus called to the cohort, "Make Rome Proud!"

Titus struggled to free himself from the huge hawthorn bush. His hands were ripped to pieces, and his tunic was snagged in multiple places, holding him fast. The momentum of his fall had plunged him completely through the bush. His head had been wrapped in a thorn-laden trailing throng, finally stopping him and boring its prongs deep into his head.

Titus had heard the noises above him. The carnyx's constant blowing, the taunting, the laughter. He even thought he could hear Fuscus's voice shouting. *Why are they pouring water?* he wondered. He had heard the shrill of the Draco and the enormous howl and roar of the wolves. Their footsteps were coming nearer at a pace. He had to release himself!

The throng wrapped around his head had its barbs latched deeply under his skin. He shut his eyes and wrestled his head to the left, ripping out the thorns and tearing his ear lobe open. Pouring with blood, he pulled with all his might, shredding his cheek, finally freeing his head. By craning his neck, he could now take in the full extent of his predicament. He raised his arms as far as he could and started to raise his chest. Gradually, at first, but increasingly, the speed and pressure paid off. The thorns holding his tunic and chest started to rip free, eventually allowing him to sit up.

Above him, a crushing sound exploded through the air. A terrifying chorus of screams accompanied by a bone-shaking crack of splintering timber. He had to get up with the first cohort. With all his strength, he leaned forward, finally tearing the thorns out from his legs and enabling him to stand up. Blood pouring from every wound, he crawled his way up the shingled slope towards the noise.

Fifteen feet from the testudo and at full speed, Moskon raised his falx. The wolf warriors followed his command, and with an almighty crash, they brought down their falx blades onto the scutum. Double-handed falxes five feet long were powerfully driven down, smashing overhead into the interlocked scutum.

Red splinters flew like sparks from an open fire grate as the blows continued to rain in. Still, the testudo retained its resilience, protected by the formation's rigidity. Wolves danced in with shorter falx, probing and hooking, trying to rip a scutum from a legionnaire's grasp. Twisting and cutting through any small crevice or left unguarded gap, they searched endlessly for any exposed hands and faces.

As the wolves moved in, the brutality of the testudo unfurled. Like a well-worn clockwork machine, it opened and closed, each motion seamless, deliberate and deadly. Screams of agony rang out all across the battlefield. Time and again, along the ranks, gladii stabbed short, sharp, and straight. Entering into exposed stomachs, they twisted free and swiftly returned behind the safety of the scutum.

Fuscus, commanding the rear guard, was scrutinising developments. The first wave of wolves had withdrawn to fifty feet. Their first attack had been ferocious, but for all its intensity, the testudo had held. A number of legionnaires had been maimed. Loss of fingers and hands, but the formation had been maintained by the efficiency of the first. Switching the injured legionnaires backward, the replacement from the second rank smoothly moved forward to the front. Back-ups from the rear guard dropped into the rear ranks, ready to take their place when required. Roman organisation at its most effective and lethal.

Moskon looked along the testudo—thirty ranks long. As he gazed, piles of wolves lay dead or dying, their guts spilt by the adept gladius. So many had been lost, he couldn't count. The howls of excitement had now turned to screams of agony. He looked at the Romans just across from him. Certainly battered, but still regimented, still disciplined, and far from any sign of capitulation. He had to break the wall!

Titus appeared behind the rear guard, having scrambled up the shingle slope and through the vegetation. He was covered in blood and looked as though he had been on the front line against the wolves. He was grabbed by a guard and immediately thrown to the ground, a gladius pinning him between his shoulder blades.

Titus shouted, " Get off me. I have to report to the Praetorian Prefect."

"Who the fuck are you?" said the guard.

"Titus Livius Decimus," he replied. "I report directly to Fuscus."

Fuscus watched as the wolves withdrew. They'd taken heavy losses. He cursed himself—such a waste of Roman life. *If only I hadn't been so foolish... rushing forward without proper preparation.* Based on the combat, he was certain the full might of his legions would have crushed them. Now, his only hope was to hold out for as long as possible. He prayed the price they were exacting from the heathens was too steep-steep enough to drive them back into the forest. Then, perhaps, he could retreat to the stronghold, regroup with fresh legions, and destroy them once and for all

Aulus Septimius stood, legs braced and arms raised within rank five of the testudo. His scutum was held tightly above his head and interlocked securely above the head of Gnaeus Petronius, standing ahead of him in the front row. Gnaeus had raised his scutum upward, creating a solid barrier. On either side of Aulus and to his rear, his comrades' scutum were fully interlocked, creating the solid testudo. A dim, stinking, man-made shell. Dingy and oppressive, punctuated only by thin shafts of light as men shifted their weight and adjusted their stance. Aulus was only able to catch a brief glimpse forward through the small gaps between the scutum.

They had been braced for over an hour, arms and legs burning from the twenty-two-pound weight of the scutum. Deep within the shell, they had heard the warriors approach, howling and shrieking. Gnaeus had caught a brief glimpse through the side of his scutum as the advanced group paraded in front of them. Wolf skin-clad and huge falxes in hand, they swaggerd past them. They had heard the taunts and laughter as they returned from their sortie.

As they pissed in front of the legionnaires, he heard someone in the ranks shout, "Their cocks are far smaller than those blades!"

The whole testudo erupted with laughter.

Gnaeus felt the first blow across his tightly held scutum, slamming hard across the curve of its surface. Made of three sheets of wood glued together, covered with canvas and leather, it was manoeuvrable, strong and extremely sturdy. Standing almost four feet high and combined with the rigidity of the surrounding interlocked shields, he was confident that it would protect him. He and Aulus had fought many battles together. Seamlessly rotating positions in the ranks, hour after hour, protecting and defending each other. Like their comrades, years of training and discipline had turned them into a formidable killing machine.

Gnaeus absorbed the blow, braced by the support of Aulus standing behind him. Now, the initial shock of the first blow had passed, his training automatically engaged, and he started to assess the incoming blows. The long falx was his biggest danger. The length of the blade and handle allowed two-handed forceful blows whilst keeping the wolf at a safe distance. The tremendous cutting force was a concern. Splinters were already flying when a clean hit was made. He found if he angled the scutum just before impact, he could minimise the damage.

Often, the glanced blow would throw the wolf off balance, and when combined with his momentum, it would almost bring him into striking distance. Gnaeus was also wary of the falx blades probing through the gaps in the scutum wall. Searching for limbs and faces, or hooking at his shield with their curved ends, trying to tear it from his grasp. A number of times, Aulus had smashed down from behind with his gladius onto the probing blade, jarring it to the floor.

The short falx was different. The wolves were still probing but also trying to sweep at the legionnaire's legs and feet, edging ever nearer. Gnaeus used Aulus support to balance, keeping his feet back and as clear as possible. Gnaeus seized his opportunity. As the short blow came in, his gladius spoke. A straight stab shot out through the briefly open scutum wall. His blow penetrated six inches, the broad blade severing multiple organs. A quick twist released the blade, instantly retreating back behind the scutum.

Gnaeus, now totally blood-stained, maintained his carnage. Blow after blow, stab after stab, a perfected rhythm of death. The screams and cries rose louder and louder, chillingly echoing through the catacomb-like chambers of the testudo

Tarbus stood at the clearing, looking towards Moskon and the devastation in front of him. He reprimanded himself, "How had the Roman bastards managed to defend themselves? How could I have been so confident in the sheer number of wolves? They had to get near them to kill them."

He heard running feet coming from behind him and quickly turned around. "Romans!" the scout shouted. "Coming down the Tapae road."

Tarbus snapped, "How many? How are they armed?"

The scout urgently replied, "Possibly four hundred men, and I counted forty or more archers."

Tarbus called to Moskon, "Withdraw fifty feet and keep them guessing on our next move."

Tarbus called out to his nephew, "Sarmis, I need four hundred wolves and you with me now!" Sarmis sprinted off to the back of the clearing and in a matter of minutes, a full group of wolves were waiting for Tarbus's command. "There are four hundred Romans and archers marching towards us. We cannot let them join up with those."

He looked across at the testudo in disgust and spat. He shouted Sarmis, "Go through the forest; surprise has to be our approach."

The group quickly vanished deep into the forest. Their knowledge of hidden paths and tracks allowing them to move swiftly through the dense, seemingly impenetrable wilderness. They had covered a quarter of a mile when they heard the Romans. These didn't seem to be legionaries, they were too noisy, lacking the discipline and order of trained troops. Tarbus pushed through a thick bush and carefully looked up the road. As he had thought, these were mainly engineers and only a few legionnaires. The archers were walking alongside the main group, ready to respond.

Tarbus quietly beckoned Sarmis forward to him and whispered, "They are more focused on the road forward. We will surprise them. Only a few have shields, and the rest look more like farmers than legionnaires. Tell your men to spread along the road a hundred yards. On my signal, attack and make them scream like your brothers have screamed."

Sextus, bloodied but strong, still stood outside of the testudo. At his feet lay dead or dying. Writhing in pain or gasping their last breath. He had, as was expected, led from the front. He was a master with the scutum and gladius. Fending off long falx blows whilst jinking and blocking the smaller falx threats, faking and drawing, he steadily drew them onto him. A single flash of gladius at the right moment, and they fell, incredulous and disembowelled. As he recovered his breath, he recalled watching his glorious first in action. Only a few had been injured, some badly, but they never stopped. Steadfast, brave, and disciplined, they had wrought dreadful damage to the swarming warrior waves.

Sextus looked over at Moskon. Behind him, thousands of wolves were spread out across the clearing, now silent. Their previous swagger dissipated. "What the fuck are they doing?" he said to the nearest legionnaire to him.

"Let them stay there all fucking night, Primus," came the reply.

Sextus smiled. He thought he could play games, too. Make their leader think. "Destruirte testudinum! Break the testudo!" he shouted at the top of his voice.

The shell parted.

He followed up with, "Be prepared in an instant."

Fuscus heard the guard speak, "Sir."

He looked at the guard and then at Titus, who was standing beside him. Blood strewn and body gauged, he could have come straight from the front line.

Fuscus said, "Titus, I heard from the Primus Pilus that you tried to warn of the ambush. A brave effort, but sadly too late." He then followed with, "Where have you been?"

Titus looked down at the ground and sheepishly said, "Stuck in a bloody thorn bush."

Fuscus and the guard both struggled to stop themselves from laughing. Titus glared at the guard, daring him to release even the smallest chuckle. Fuscus coughed heavily, trying his best to hide his amusement.

"Well," he said, "I am glad you are back with us now. We need every man. By the way, where is that bloody dog of yours?"

CHAPTER 8:
Dog Number Four

Hidden in a thicket, a hundred yards behind the wolves, Lakon licked his wounds. His rampaging through the wolf warriors, although successful, hadn't been totally one-sided. Although he had caused huge damage, tearing and ripping at men as he surged along the track, a couple of blows had caught him. A dagger had sliced high across his shoulder, and a wild swing of a falx had cut the tip off his ear. Although bleeding, he had suffered far worse throughout his life.

Now, though, the pain that surged through him was greater than anything he had felt. He had lost the only being who had truly cared for him, Titus.

Following his attack on the wolves, he ran on for a short while and then quickly circled back to the edge of the forest clearing. As he reached the clearing, he saw Titus strike down the second Wolf warrior and then charge down the slope, immediately followed by another towering warrior. As the Wolf was about to strike, a legionary's spear spiked his neck, hurling him backwards. Titus in his haste tripped and was sent sprawling forward onto the road, landing at the feet of a group of legionnaires. As he was helped to his feet, the legionnaire nearest to him was hit by an immense log. It slammed them both into the air, somersaulting across the road and over the edge of the mountain.

Eyes heavy and distant, Lakon slumped to the floor, the weight of grief and exhaustion finally closing in upon him. A faint whimper escaped, followed by a deep sigh that rose from his blood-soaked chest. In that moment, surrounded by the echoes of battle and the stench of death, a deep sorrow enclosed him like a shroud, heavy and unyielding.

Lakon was born among a litter destined for violence. As Canis Molossus, they were bred only as tools for profit and war. Crossbred and selected from only the strongest and most aggressive, they were designed to become massive, muscular, and fearsome beasts. Lakon's life was ordained for brutality.

Janius Firmus believed that harsh treatment produced fiercer dogs. Lakon was separated from his mother early and thrust into a squalid cage. A slender, rusted chain collar, cruelly spiked, encircled his neck, its rough metal ceaselessly chafing the skin beneath. He was disciplined and tormented daily by heavy blows from a switch and constant kicking. To Janius's delight, at eight months, he was developing into a fearful beast, worthy of a heavy price.

In spring, the travelling fairs arrived in the blossoming Spanish countryside. Acrobats, dancers, and strong men paraded proudly through the streets. Sights, sounds, and smells from every exotic part of the Roman Empire gathered to celebrate the passing of the winter. Scantily dressed women with sparkling white veils appeared to float and dance along the streets. Their intoxicating perfume filled the air, as they smiled and teased the excited young men watching them. Expert horsemen dressed in vivid orange uniforms were riding powerful and elegant jet black stallions. Their fiery red eyes, wild and alert, scanned the noisy and boisterous crowd. They bucked and kicked out, forcing the onlookers to keep their distance. One rider was standing on the backs of two horses, two reins in hand. He performed acrobatics whilst harnessing the thoroughbred's power. Within the parade, a strongman strutted and swaggered along the street. He teased and taunted the wide-eyed young men who watched in awe as he performed feats of strength and sheer power.

The parade rolled into the town square, and immediately, a hive of activity erupted. The building of tents and stalls, buskers calling, and music echoing off the buildings all combined into a cacophony of sound. Smoke started to rise from every corner, as the street vendors quickly lit their open fires. Soon, the tantalising aroma of exotic dishes drifted through the air. Sizzling meats and roasted corn, enticing all who passed by.

Behind the flamboyant face of the fair lay its grimy underbelly. Enticing, dangerous, and yet so exhilarating and exciting. Caestus boxers wearing metal-studded leather gloves fought each other to a standstill. Great wounds would be inflicted as they pounded each other senseless. Faces erupting, ribs fracturing, they staggered and swore, trying to land the killer blow.

However, as much of a spectacle as the Caestus was, the greatest attraction at the fair was the dog fights. A man could win or lose a small fortune in the space of minutes.

The travelling fighting pit had been made from old amphorae boxes stacked into a circle. Standing five feet high, its sides were stained with the blood of a thousand fights. A lasting testimony to the slaughter and lives sacrificed. For the victor, momentary reprieve; for the loser, death. There was no escape.

The travellers were renowned for their dog breeding. They brought their best and most ferocious each year. Fit and ready to pit against the region's champions. Excitement, expectation, and trepidation filled the air!

Janius had been excited about the forthcoming spring fair for many months. He had been diligent over the years, and his kennel of fearsome dogs had grown in size and reputation. His methods in producing winners, although unorthodox, had been successful. His dog had savaged the travellers champion last year, leaving it crippled. Its body was found in a ditch on the eastern road. If you can't fight, you have no value and food costs money.

Janius didn't give his dogs a name. They were purely business assets. There was no space for names or sentimentality. This year, *Number One Dog* had developed well. It had gained considerable muscle, increasing to a colossal one hundred and forty pounds in weight. Janius had continued to 'educate' the dog. His successful routine of torment, regular beatings, and pain developed character! At this time of year, the stray dog population in the town would dramatically decline. *Number One* had been pitted against these starving wretches, ripping them apart within minutes of being thrown into the training pit.

Janius was confident of victory this year. Over the last months, he had shown many of the town's traders and merchants *Number One*. They had seen its ferocity and mercilessness in the pit. Nothing could match the power and strength the dog possessed. Within the last few days, many side bets from the rich, powerful, and unscrupulous members of society had been placed on his dog. He was going to make them a lot of money. No more Janius the dog beater. The favours he would be owed would allow his place in society to be elevated, making him a rich man.

Fausto silently climbed up onto the yard wall. Under the light of the full moon, he could clearly make out the kennels. He mused, *With the stench of this place, I could have found it in the pitch dark.*

He carefully crept along the wall towards the kennels. There could be no noise to wake up the dogs. On his back was a large leather sack, fastened by straps around his waist. He could feel his back becoming wetter as the blood oozed and seeped out of the sack. He stopped and listened, checking for any sounds. All was still. He could see the four dilapidated cages twenty yards away, the smell now almost overpowering him. He pulled up the scarf from around his neck and secured it across his nose. He was pleased with himself and all his efforts: his plan was working.

He had spent the early evening in the tavern, listening to the conversations. *Number One* was the only subject on people's minds. How long would the fight last? What would be left of the other dog when it was over? There was no doubt in anyone's minds about the result.

At the centre of attention was an old man. He appeared to know more about the dog than anyone. On listening closer, he found out that he was the night watchman of the kennels. Fasuto carefully made his play. Many drinks later, Fausto watched the old man leave the tavern, swaying as he walked out through the door. Fausto waited a few minutes, then said his goodbyes to the other revellers and left the tavern. He quickly caught up with the old man in his drunken state, and helped him stumble back towards the kennel. He fumbled for the keys in his pocket and, with Fausto's help, unlocked it and pushed open the door. The old man mumbled and pointed to his bed. Fausto walked him across to his bed and started to help the old man lie down.

As the old man thankfully lay down, a dagger ran across his throat, his breath leaving him with staggering gasps. Fausto held his hand over his mouth and gently let the dying man down. He took the keys and quietly retraced his steps to the gate. Checking that the street was empty, he stepped through, turned and locked the gate, then dropped the keys back on the inside of the yard.

Fausto was now above the cages. Still, there was no disturbance from the dogs below. He swung the leather sack around and slit the straps with his dagger. He put his hand inside and felt the clammy dampness of the raw meat squeeze between his fingers. Carefully, he drew out the first lump of meat and dropped it into the first cage. Still no noise! As with the first, he stealthily dropped a parcel down into the remaining three cages. His mission completed, he retraced his steps along the wall and waited. Within minutes he could hear the slurping and chomping of the dogs as they consumed his precious gift. Fausto's face broke into a huge smile, his gold tooth, glinted in the moonlight. Carefully he continued back along the wall and silently hung down and dropped to the floor.

He had liked the old man and felt a slight tinge of remorse. He knew that there was a chance he could have seen Fausto on the wall. The only way he could dispatch the meat silently without the dogs barking was from above them and then drop it down into the cages. Fausto shrugged and then silently disappeared into the night.

Janius woke up with a start. Today was the day. At last, all the years of struggling, being a lowly citizen, would be behind him. The slate would be wiped clean. He would buy a fine house on Main Street, have servants provide for his every wish. He could run for the local council and be a lawmaker. He smiled at the thought, *Janius, a law-abiding citizen!*

He strode out of his front door, heading down the dirty alleyway that led to the kennels. Even at this distance, he could smell the rancid meat and dog faeces. His neighbours never complained. They knew better! The discovery of the fisherman found with his throat cut, previously seen arguing with Janius, still remained unresolved, unproven.

The sun was just rising as he reached the kennel, it was going to be a beautiful day. The old man would have risen earlier, checked all the cages, and opened the gate. As it was fight day, the dogs had been starved for twenty-four hours. He wanted them ravenous, their primeval instincts to the fore.

Janius pushed the gate, but it wouldn't move. He pushed it harder, but still, it wouldn't budge. "That fucking old bastard is pissed again," he said." I'm going to wring his neck. On a day like today, too!"

Janius reached for his belt and pulled off his own set of keys. Slipping the key in, he turned the lock and pushed. The gate swung open, and there, lying on the ground two feet in front of him, was the old man's set of keys.

Janius called the man. Silence. He called again- nothing. Just silence. There was something missing. His brain struggled to comprehend the situation. Then the realisation set in. There was no barking!

He ran to the kennels, the pungent stench hitting his senses like a wave. He approached *Number One's* cage.

Lying at the back of the cage, it lay. Tongue out, white foam streaming from its mouth, and a pool of yellow bile surrounding its enormous, bloated body. Janius, yelling, ran to the next cage. The same scene greeted him. He went to the third and found the animal dragging itself around the cage, vomiting yellow bile and biting itself in distress. As Janius opened the cage, the animal flew at the door, teeth bared and snarling, with white foam frothing across its mouth. As it reached the door, it collapsed, its breath coming in huge spasms. As Janius watched, the creature writhed in agony, its whole body shaking. A final almighty spasm shook the beast, its bowels expelled, and the dog died.

Janius fell to his knees and screamed. All his dreams had been destroyed overnight. No longer a prominent citizen, no fine house on Main Street. So many people who would lose their money. He would be hated and worse.

He ran to the old man's shelter at the corner of the yard. There he lay, throat slit. Eyes wide open amid a pool of blood.

His brain went into a whirl. What could he do? Should he run, hide in the countryside? Leave his home and abandon his whole life's work? He considered so many options. Some of the people could afford the loss. Others would not forgive, and if he could not pay, they would find another way to make him. Janius fell to the floor, grabbed a handful of soil, and sobbed.

From cage number four, he heard a noise! He jumped to his feet and sprinted across the yard. As he reached the cage, he was rushed by a blaze of black, fangs bared, spit dripping, and eyes so wild like a devil. *Dog Number Four*, the giant juvenile, was alive! How?

Janius looked around the cage. A pit of filth, faeces, and decaying meat was the creature's home. Clumps of hair were entrapped on the bars, where the dog had rubbed itself raw from the irritation of the fleas and ticks swarming its body.

In the corner, high on the top bars, a lump of raw meat hung by the thinnest sliver of skin, swaying precariously. It had clearly been caught when being dropped and was just high enough to have evaded the dog standing up at full stretch.

Janius quickly ran to his shack and picked up a wire lasso. A six-foot pole with a wide loop fixed at the end. Inside, a lasso was attached around the loop, and a length of rope ran back to the end of the pole. He then picked up a sturdy leather muzzle and loosely secured it to his belt. He ran to the cage where the dog was still barking and growling. Undoing the bolt slowly, he opened the door enough to push the pole through.

Slowly, he pushed the dog backwards and edged himself into the cage.

The dog backed up to the side bars and then stood its ground. Hackles raised, its mouth drawn back, exposing huge canine teeth. Slowly, Janius edged forward, elevating the pole and wire loop above the dog's head. The dog watched intently as, step by step, Janius positioned the loop just above its head. It took a quick step to the right, sensing the danger, but Janius was too quick. A master at his trade, he swooped the loop down over the dog's enormous head and, with a quick tug on the rope, the noose tightened around its neck. Instantly, Janius tugged hard on the rope, pulling the stunned dog across the cage and tying it tightly head first onto the bars of the cage. Deftly, he pulled the leather muzzle off his belt. With practised expertise, he avoided the snarling teeth, rammed it over the dog's snout, and secured the buckles. The dog, now restrained on the bars, shook its body with all its might. Hard as it tried to free itself, it was held fast.

Janius walked to the back of the cage, reached up, and pulled down the now stinking piece of meat. He walked out of the cage, still cautiously watching the dog. He grabbed a shovel, dug a hole in the yard, and threw the poison package in, covering it and tamping the surface down smooth.

Janius slowly walked over to the cages, surveying the dreadful scene. Lying there were his three most prized dogs. Poisoned! His business lay in tatters. Anger surged through him. Whoever did this, they will pay dearly!

He stood and assessed the situation. In retrospect, he realised that there were too many candidates. His entire business had been built on unscrupulous practices, never afraid to cross the line when necessary: whether through physical threats, coercion of any kind, or outright bribery. He reviewed his exposure. There was a small fortune of bets placed that would have to be honoured. His dream of a better life lay in tatters. Gone was the fabulous house, the servants, the prestige.

From the cage, dog number four made a subdued growl, still aggressively shaking its body, trying to free itself. Janius's anger left him and a wry smile spread across his face. He looked across at the beast; it was a powerhouse of a dog, full of spite and hate. *It might just work. Could he?* he wondered. It would be a huge challenge up against the travellers champion. What did he have to loose? It was just a juvenile, unproven in a fight, but there was no mistaking its quality or its formidable bloodline.

In the evening darkness, the pit had been lit by oil lamps, casting eerie shadows that danced around the stone courtyard walls. As ever, there was an atmosphere of expectation and carnival. Fire grates, with meat slowly cooking, smoked and spat. Wine sellers were doing a mighty trade, ensuring their rich clients' glasses were continuously full. For the poor revellers, posca traders served a continuous demand for their vinegar beverage. A far cheaper alternative to wine, but still packing a punch.

The courtyard was filled shoulder to shoulder. Not a spare space to be found. The atmosphere was high with anticipation for the final fight. Vast sums had been wagered on both beasts; for many, dreams or devastation hung in the balance." The first four fights had been disappointing, with the favourites subduing and dispatching their opponent in quick fashion. In the previous fight, the two dogs were well matched. They engaged ferociously, ripping at each other's faces. Countering and attacking equally. Finally, the slightly larger dog managed to gain an advantage, tightening its hold around the other dog's throat until it dropped to the floor unconscious. The winning owner ran into the pit and prised the dog's jaws away, dragging it back to its tether. The unconscious dog's owner dragged it from the ring by its hind legs and flung it like an old sack into a small travelling cage on his cart.

The crowd suddenly parted, and Fausto entered the courtyard, leading a huge crossbred. The dog's fur was a dirty brown, except for a large white spot across its back. As it strutted heavily into the pit, its neck and shoulders rippled and bulged like a gladiatorial prize fighter. The muzzle on his face barely managed to retain the animal's huge, scared face. As it walked along, it snarled and growled angrily at the nearby crowd. Fausto followed his prize possession, proudly taking up his position in the pit. He had not heard any news from the town gossips following his nighttime activities. He smiled, this was going to be easy. Their match had been set on open rules. No show meant defeat, and he could collect all his winnings. Fausto confidently looked around the crowd, waiting calmly, expecting Janius not to show and a defeat to be declared.

He pulled hard on his dogs leash as it jumped forward, excited by a huge roar from the local partisan crowd. They hated the traveller breeders and took every opportunity to show it. Fausto's smile instantly disappeared as he turned his head and looked towards the entrance. Standing and smiling stood Janius, holding the leash of a monster Canis Molossus. He could see it was a juvenile, but what a fine specimen. Janius looked at Fausto, looked at his dog, and spat on the ground.

Never had the crowd seen such a pairing of prime specimens. They cheered and roared, exploding with impatient anticipation. Frenzied placement of last-minute bets was screamed across the courtyard.

Glasses were refilled, and finally, the noise abated. The fight was set.

The two owners struggled to retain the beasts as they manhandled them into position. Both dogs were standing on their hind legs, growling ferociously. Heckles rose, spittle dripping out through their muzzles into large pools on the ground. Janius and Fusto were big men, but so intense were the dogs pulling that they both called for seconds to help hold them apart.

When the starter climbed up onto his platform, the excitement of the crowd exploded to boiling point. White flag in hand, he slowly raised his arm high above his head. Shouting at the top of his voice, he shouted, "Release muzzles."

The owners gingerly removed them, the dogs' snarling and growling intensifying as their jaws became free. He then slowly started his countdown, "Three, Two…"

On two, Fausto and his second released their dog. The beast sprinted across towards *Number Four*, still retained. He hit the dog, Janius, and his second at full speed, knocking all three over. It immediately pounced on the toppled dog, searching for its throat. Teeth snapping and biting, it used its powerful shoulders and front legs to try and pull *Number Four* closer.

The partisan crowd jeered as the beast pressed forward. Janius and his second rolled clear, sprinting to the pit wall and vaulting over. *Number Four* regained his senses and used his immense strength to get to his feet. The brown beast lunged again, just missing his throat. *Number Four* took three steps back and then launched an almighty charge, hitting the brown dog with all his immense weight. The impact knocked it heavily sideways into the ring side walls.

Number Four darted forwards with all his weight, pinning the dog against the sideboards, and started to rip at its neck. Whelps of pain screeched from the dog's mouth. Huge canine teeth tore into the soft tissue, ripping chunks away as it bit and thrashed its head. He momentarily released his vice-like grip. The brown dog, sensing the change of pressure, instantly ripped itself free and charged into the centre of the ring. It turned and faced the fearsome sight of *Number Four*. Teeth bared, eyes wild, with blood and saliva pouring from its mouth.

The dog had fought many times, its body showing the signs of its victories. Multiple scars across its face and shoulders bore witness to his battles. It had always been supreme. Often hurt, it always had the power and aggression to turn the fight. Finally dominating and securing a locked jaw on his opponent's throat, ripping and throttling it into unconsciousness.

This was different; he had never experienced such power, such aggression. For the first time in his life, he was scared.

Fausto sensed the change in his champion. The aggression that he always portrayed seemed to be subsiding. The pack nature of a more powerful hierarchy was setting in. Soon it would be all over.

Number Four sensed it, too. Thousands of years of evolution were hard-wired into him. He knew he was the more dominant of the two. His opponent knew it also. It would only be a matter of time before the dog lay on his back, whimpering, ears flattening, and acknowledging him as pack leader by licking his face.

The crowd gasped as they saw the black devil gather himself, focus, and prepare to launch an almighty leap towards his victim.

Number Four charged at the inferior animal. Teeth snarling, eyes set, he aimed his full body weight at the soon-to-be subservient dog. An outright display of superiority.

The power and force of the collision were incredible. The impact sent both dogs spinning and barrelling apart. The brown dog let out an incredible whimpering screech, whilst Number Four howled in knowing triumph. The whole crowd turned and looked at the whimpering dog. A champion they had seen destroy many opponents previously was now totally submissive.

The crowd reached fever pitch. Screaming, shouting, laughing, and cursing. Never had they seen such a display of dominance from any dog. Certainly not a juvenile. This must be the champion of all champions in the making.

The momentum of the clash drove Number Four rolling to the perimeter of the pit. He stood up and looked across at his foe. The dog now trembling, urinated and it sunk to the floor. Number took a step back and his flanks touch the pit side panels. Without warning, a sharp, stabbing pain pierced him. Fausto's stiletto knife, fixed under his sleeve, penetrated between his ribs into his lung. So expert was the move, the crowd saw nothing more than a man pushing a dog aside.

Number Four felt lightheaded and weak. The air was seeping from his lungs, his bullish strength slowly ebbing away.

Janius was jumping up and down, slapping the backs of his newfound friends. As promised, his dog had provided them with a healthy profit. He was going to be the toast of the town.

Out in the pit, the whimpering dog sensed a change. He looked towards Number Four; his eyes were dull, and the fire had gone. It had not come in for the final kill.

Instantly, it was revitalised. Confidence regained, power and strength surged back through its body. A low growl grew from the depths of its throat, turning into a haunting howl. It charged across the pit, towards the staggering Number Four.

Before the crowd could comprehend the change, it had grabbed its foe. Ripping and tearing every part of its body, it could bite. It was only the pure bulk of Number Four's body that allowed him to keep his throat out of reach.

The partisan crowd, who had tasted victory briefly, jumped to their feet, shouting and hollering. They all turned to look at Janius. Now, a shadow of the man he was two minutes ago.

Fausto cleverly jumped into the pit and dragged his champion away from Number Four. He could see the damage from so many bites, and the streams of blood pouring from the dog's body that hid the critical, tiny puncture his stiletto had made. The listless body of Number Four lay panting and dying on the dirt floor of the pit.

Oh, how the crowd had turned! All Janius could now hear was the crowd baying for his blood. He had promised them a champion. He had convinced them all that it was a sure bet. Now, he had put a juvenile dog in the pit. It clearly wasn't strong enough to fight. He had cheated them.

Janius grabbed the tether rope and tied it around Number Four's waist. He dragged the dying dog out of the pit and into the back of the courtyard to his cart. With the help of his second, they winched the limp body up onto his cart. Janius had only one thought. *Escape.*

With the noise of the crowd growing angrier in his ears, he whipped the mule hard. The animal shuddered and pulled the cart out of the courtyard at a pace. Janius had to get to the kennels and collect a few treasured things. He would then leave this festering town for good.

He heard the dog whimper, and his anger exploded. Number Four was still breathing, but he was of no value to Janius. He stopped the cart, grabbed the rope still attached around the beast's waist, and with a mighty heave, hauled the limp beast's body onto the street. He dragged it into the gutter, followed by a huge kick. Angrily, he climbed back onto the cart.

Titus was off duty in the town when the courtyard exploded. As a member of the Praetorian Guard, he rushed towards the noise to find out what the issue was. He was faced with total uproar. The pit had turned into a mass brawl. Gamblers, traders, travellers - punching, kicking, swearing. Wine, posca, and food were being thrown. Cries of: "Fix," "Cheats," "Where is my money?" rang out.

Titus laughed and under his breath said, "Spring Fair."

Leaving them to their quarrels, he walked out the side gate and down the back lane. He knew this area well. He also knew the stench from the kennels he would have to walk past. He drew close, now almost gagging from the stench. He didn't remember it being as bad as this. In front of him in the gloom of the alley, he could see what appeared to be a huge black sack. As he got closer, the features of a massive dog became clearer. He stopped; it looked dead. He presumed another innocent victim of the dog fights. He was just about to walk on when he heard the whimper. The dog was alive. Barely, but still alive.

He took a closer look. He could now make out, under the dim light, that it was an enormous Canis Molossus. Still a juvenile, but enormous. As a boy on his father's farm, they had kept them to protect his goats and cattle. He carefully ran his hands over its blood-soaked body. He could feel a mass of bites, still seeping blood. There were none on his throat, and the others, although severe, were not bad enough to have dropped a dog of his size.

Titus held the huge head of the dog in his hands. Its eyes slowly opened, and they locked with his own. A stare looking for compassion. He felt some unexplainable connection to the beast embrace him.

If he could get it back to the barracks, the years of watching and helping his mother heal and tend to the wounds of their animals, he might just be able to save its life.

Janius arrived at the gates and drove the cart into the open gates, the stench of the three dead dogs now overpowering the usual fetid odour. Janius walked behind the stinking cages to a locked shed. He drew out a key and unlocked the door. Quickly, he lit an oil lamp, barely lifting the gloom. He had stashed some jewels won in a previous fight behind a loose rock. Fumbling, he found the rock. He picked them up and held them up to the lamp light. They gleamed and sparkled in the dim orange light of the flame. They would help him start a new life.

Janius didn't hear the silent footsteps. He briefly felt the dagger go across his throat. His last gasp of breath was only heard by Fausto!

CHAPTER 9:
The White Marble Villa

Decimus had heard the raw chaos of battle as he and his group marched down the road. The carnyx calling, the clash of men, shouting, swearing, and the screaming of stricken men. It had started with the occasional outburst and steadily grown into a cacophony of suffering.

Decimus had for many years witnessed the efficiency of the legions firsthand. Although he had completed his basic legion training as all entrants had to do, his skills as an engineer had shone through. He quickly advanced through the ranks, rising to Praefectus Fabrum.

His rank had allowed him to be at the forefront of most campaigns. Whether in the construction of attack towers or, as in the case of this campaign, roads and bridges ahead of the Vanguard. He always had a grandstand view of the efficiency and subsequent destruction a legion in full combat mode could deliver.

He knew from his campaign experience that if sufficient men had survived and they had the appropriate weapons available, a well-organised defence could hold out for many hours. The first cohort, in his opinion, had the best Primus Pilus of all the legions. Sextus, if alive, would have them so well organised that it would take a gifted general to break them down.

Decimus knew that the whole group would be safer under Sextus's command. It was critical for his men to get through and add to whatever numbers remained. Decimus shouted, "Keep the pace up. We have to join them, it's our only hope."

Tarbus looked along the line of warriors, hidden along the edge of the trees. He mouthed to Sarmis, *'Take out the archers first.'*

Sarmis nodded and silently spread the word amongst the group. He knew they would have to be quick. Unless they removed the threat of the archers, they would lose too many men. Surprise would be the only way to take them out.

Sarmis gave the order. Along the line of hidden warriors, fifty men detached their slings from their belts. Each had a bag of stones that had been shaped and smoothed and now resembled small eggs. The size and weight were perfect for accuracy and to deliver as much impact at short range. They quietly moved forward to the edge of the forest and squatted down, hidden in the long grass.

The Roman group came into view, marching at pace. These weren't legionnaires drilled to perfection. Some were out of step, some with their shoulders rolling side to side, an energy-sapping effort. Not the efficiency of a true legionnaire. But they were big men. Years of heavy engineering, road building, and tree felling had turned them into powerful men. Huge shoulders, massive biceps, and solid, tree-trunk legs. In a street fight, you wouldn't bet against any of them.

On the outside of the group, the archers were keeping pace. Each one had an arrow notched in his bow, watching warily as they moved through the forest. A quiver of arrows was slung at a low level, secured by their left legs. Its positioning was critical, allowing the fast retrieval of the next arrow as soon as they had loosed their shot. In battle, they could accurately fire three or four arrows in a minute, creating a shower of death.

Caius Fabii was a master Sagittarii, with fifteen years' service. He had fought in many campaigns throughout the empire. He commanded the fifty archers. They respected his skills as a fellow archer and trusted his clear-headed leadership when under attack. On many occasions, his steady hand and keen eye had been a major factor in their success. The speed and accuracy of his shots made him a formidable assaillant.

Caius walked alongside the front of the group. Decimus was to his left, cajoling and cursing his group of engineers, driving them forward. Decimus looked out to his right and the forest edge. He knew it was perfect ambush territory. There was no other route. They had no choice but to walk the path that fate had brought them on.

Decimus quietly spoke to Caius, "Be prepared. You and your men are the only link between life and death for us all."

Caius replied, "I've got twenty arrows. Everyone has a wolf bastard's name on it. They are going to have to run like the wind to get through to us."

Tucked away in the trees, Sarmis had nimbly worked his way right to the end of the line of slingers. Quietly encouraging, he ordered them to hold their fire until his command. They were all set and ready for action.

The Romans marched past Sarmis's hiding place, pushing hard. Their eyes totally focused, staring ahead. Their goal was to reach the huge tree trunks blocking the way to the stricken cohort. Yet it was still half a mile away. Sarmis sensed they knew their fate. One slight chance to connect with their comrades and a last stand with the eagle.

As the last rank of the engineers walked by Sarmis, he gave the command. The fifty slingers along the line rose from their hiding places. They had previously placed their first stone into the leather pouches at the centre of the sling. Fixed on either side of the pouch was a two-foot-long thin strip of leather. Grasping the two ends in their hands, they twirled them around their heads. As the speed increased, they angled the pouch, aimed at their chosen target and released the stone.

The stones flew out with such speed and precision, their intended targets were oblivious of the incoming danger. All along the marching line, archers dropped to their knees. Their bows flying up into the air and flailing, hiting the engineers walking alongside them. Some were instantly killed by a stone to the temple. Some were felled by brutal blows to the head, others by shots to the chest or legs, every strike calculated to disable.

When they missed their intended target entirely, the marching engineers in line with them went down, suffering the same savage impacts as their comrades.

Caius heard the whistle. The stone fractionally missed his head, tearing into the head of an enormous engineer between Decimus and himself. The engineer fell to his feet as blood poured out of the wound in his temple. Both he and Decimus had instantly thrown themselves onto the floor, tucking behind the frame of the engineer. His broad shoulders now provided cover and a barricade.

Caius reacted as he had been trained. The bow had been fully tensioned, and the already notched arrow was ready to be aimed. Caius waited for the next volley of stones to fly in. All around him, stunned engineers dropped. Some silently, others, their massive hands holding head wounds pouring with blood and screaming in agony.

As the volley passed, Caius popped up above the dead engineer. His trained eye allowed him to spot two slingers a hundred feet away from him. He had released one arrow, notched another, and let it fly, as the first arrow hit a wolf slinger straight in the chest. In a split second, the other arrow also hit its mark. Both wolves screamed and fell back amongst the waiting warriors. Caius dropped back behind Decimus.

He turned to Decimus and said, "After the next volley, when I fire, you check how many archers are still alive."

Decimus nodded and prepared.

The stones flew in. This time, they were not as effective as the first two volleys. Most of the engineers had dived, spread eagled onto the road, and were doing their best to shelter behind their dead comrades. The stones hit the stricken bodies with a sickening thud.

Both Caius and Decimus jumped to their feet. Caius efficiently dispatched a further two arrows. As a master archer, not a shot was ever wasted. Decimus quickly surveyed the situation and dropped back onto the ground beside Caius.

Decimus reported, "It's Bad. There were maybe ten or eleven archers left firing. A lot of casualties. The volleys have taken a number of my men down, too."

They both looked at each other. The realisation of their situation was only too clear.

Caius broke the silence, "They will attack after the next couple of volleys. They will have assessed how quickly they can get to us across the gap and how many men they may lose from my men's arrows. Prepare yourself, Decimus. It will be quick."

Decimus grabbed Caius's wrist and gave a knowing nod. No words were required.

Sarmis had seen the first volleys fly and the devastation to the Romans they had caused. Archers had dropped like flies, reducing the firepower of the group considerably. He judged that there were only ten still able to fire. He had run down the line to meet with Tarbus. Sarmis looked at Tarbus expectantly.

Tarbus nodded and said, "It's time to finish it."

Sarmis turned towards the line and gave out an almighty 'howl.' Instantly, it was replied to. As the howls reverberated, four hundred wolves rose from their hidden positions in the undergrowth and started to charge towards the Roman engineers.

Caius jumped up. He had fourteen arrows in his quiver. He was going to make them pay. He looked across the clearing. Four hundred wolves falx in hand, howling and hooting, sprinted across the clearing. His world turned into slow motion. He released arrow after arrow at the approaching hordes. From the corner of his eye, he saw two huge wolf warriors. Their wolf skins were spectacular, and they were clearly high-ranking commanders. They were arriving fast, and he only had moments left. He aimed at the older, higher-ranking wolf and gently released his fingers from the bow string. The arrow flew out straight and true. Caius allowed himself a smile. If their Chief went down, the rest might well break ranks. As he watched the arrows trajectory, the younger of the two changed direction and crossed infront of the path of the older wolf. The arrow penetrated his neck and he flew backwards, his arms flailing and dropping to the ground.

"Fuck," spilled out from Caius. He knew it was too late. The older wolf had spotted him. A short falx was already in mid-air, striking Caius straight in the chest.

As Caius fell to his knees, the last thing he heard was a swish in the air, and his head left his shoulders. The wolf howled.

Decimus had witnessed the whole scene. He was ten feet behind Caius. His old gladius from his training days in hand. He and it had never really struck a blow in anger! He stood prepared with no shield for protection. He was a Roman and proud to die for the empire.

The Chief saw him and approached, long-handled falx in hand. Decimus saw the giant wolf warrior grin and jump. He cleared the gap between them easily. Now in striking distance, he raised the four-foot-long blade and brought it down hard towards Decimus' head. Whether it was his old training or instinct for survival, his gladius was positioned perfectly to block the blow and glance it downward. As he pulled his gladius away, he swung it diagonally out in front of him and to his surprise, it slashed the wolf's left shoulder. The wolf didn't flinch but took a step backward out of range.

Adjusting his balance, a second powerful, long-range blow was driven towards Decimus. Again, it was blocked by a cross chest counter, the gladius reverberating in Decimus's right hand. The force of the blow was so powerful that it drove his arm into his chest, his own gladius trapped. The wolf looked him straight in the eyes, and with speed unexpected for such a big man, he rotated the blade in his wrist and cut down deep into Decimus's neck.

Decimus gasped with shock as blood poured from him. He bravely raised his Gladius, aiming tamely again at the wolf. It was easily parried, and a final blow straight through his stomach knocked him to the floor.

Decimus lay gasping for breath and coughing blood. With difficulty, he slowly turned his head. As he looked along the road, he could see the wolves slashing and stabbing at those who remained on their feet. One by one, they bravely fell until the entire group had been slaughtered. Sporadic howling started until they all aligned in one single voice.

Decimus closed his eyes. He saw his friends standing in a beautiful villa with long white marble columns. They stood in their immaculate white togas, smiling and waving at him. They were calling him, but he couldn't quite hear them. Then he heard on the wind, "Welcome home."

CHAPTER 10:
The Precipice

The last remnants of sunlight bled into the deepening sky, while shadows from the vast trees stretched long and soft. Dusk was settling, casting a veiled glow over the landscape, a time of quiet transition, where day surrendered to night in an unhurried embrace.

Not for Fuscus. He had heard the almighty howl coming from the Tapae road. It could have only been Decimus and his engineering party. They were the only advanced group. He groaned. Five hundred Roman engineers, with only a small protection unit. A total slaughter! A pang of guilt hit his stomach as he replayed his dreadful decisions. He regretted the cost in lives they had caused.

Fuscus' mind jolted back as he heard: "Facite testudinem!" hollered by Sextus. He looked to the front as the testudo was efficiently restored. Staring through the early evening gloom, he could make out why Sextus had issued the command. A large party of wolves had rejoined with the main group. Their whooping and howling resounded through the air as they celebrated their slaughter. Fuscus gasped in horror as he saw, high on top of a Draco pole, the head of Decimus. They paraded it amongst themselves, mocking and taunting. Its now soulless eyes, looking out towards his condemned comrades.

Titus looked at Fuscus and could see the strain in his face. The weight of the world on his shoulders. Even if it was not shown or said, the blame for this disaster was placed squarely on his head. Titus thought back to his meeting with him and their conversation. How things had changed in such a short space of time. From the confidence of a conquering empire to the tattered remnants of once mighty legions. His personal mission all but forgotten.

Titus's heart sank when he thought of Lakon. The dog had rampaged through the wolves, savaging and ripping at as many as he could. He had bravely created a diversion to allow him the opportunity to try and warn the legion. Surely he could not have survived? He had failed, and Lakon had lost his life. A deep sadness gripped him, and he fought to hide his tears.

Sextus called to Titus, " I need good men like you up here with me. Arm yourself and come stand with me. If we are going to die, let's die like true Roman legionnaires."

Titus sprang forward, picked up a gladius and sequestered a scutum from the last rank of the flank guard. He thought, *If they get around here, we are done for anyway.*

Titus ran forward and stood by the side of Sextus, set in defence mode. Sextus nodded towards the testudo, but Titus shook his head and said, " If I'm going to die, it will be by your side. Not inside some stinking chamber."

Sextus smiled, then said, "For honour and for Rome."

As Titus set himself for battle, they both heard footsteps coming from behind them and turned quickly. Fuscus was walking towards them, his commander's cloak swaying in the wind. The white plumes on his helmet stood erect, signalling him out as the field commander. There would be no hiding.

Fuscus walked up beside Sextus and said, "For honour and for Rome."

Sextus looked at the Praetorian Prefect; his demeanour had totally changed. No longer dejected or downtrodden, but the trained combatant, confident and prepared to lead. Sextus replied, "The field is yours, Prefect."

Fuscus discarded his robe, set himself with gladius and scutum in hand and replied, "The field is mine, Primus."

Across on the other side of the clearing, the carnyx rang out a series of blasts. Moskon called to his wolves, who were standing off from the testudo. They turned and ran back to the main group waiting in the forest clearing.

Tarbus spoke, "We have slaughtered the Roman engineers and archers. My scouts report that the Tapae road is now clear of all the Roman bastards. They are lying rotting, and their blood will purge the ground of their stench. I swore an oath to King Decebalus. I said we would wipe every trace of them from our sacred lands. I have lost a son and a nephew. You have all lost loved ones. Brothers, they now happily run with the wolves forever. Our task is near completion. These last Roman scum must be defeated. We cannot, we must not fail. Run with me now, and if I fall, do not stop, do not falter. Brothers, fulfill my oath. You know that one day, we will all run with the wolves forever."

Vezinas, the high priest, raised the Draco and howled. The whole throng responded in unison. High in the air atop the Draco, Decimus's lifeless eyes stared blankly down at their fervent cries.

Darkness was falling fast, and rows of fires were being lit by the wolves. As the flames grew, the light slowly lit the canopies of the trees, bathing the ground in dancing light and undulating shadows. Moskon shouted, "Build those fires high. I want the light to shine the way. I want them to see us coming, I want to see the fear in their eyes as they die."

He looked around the clearing, as multitudes of wolf silhouettes filled the space. Tarbus shouted, "Bring forward the logs and light them."

Teams of ten wolves each moved forward from the rear of the clearing, carrying ten-foot-long logs. Each had been stripped of its branches, apart from points where they now became handles. Each log had one tip placed in the fire, quickly catching alight in the intense heat.

Tarbus called Moskon over and said, "Once they are ready, we strike. Prepare the men."

In the front rank of the testudo, Aulus said to Gnaeus, "What the *fuck's* happening. What can you see?"

Gnaeus peered through the slit above the scutum, then replied, "They have lit huge fires. The sky is lighting up. I can see thousands of the bastards now."

He laughed and said, "Aulus, I think we might be here for a while!"

Aulus briefly shifted the weight from his shoulders to the top of Gnaeus's scutum, whilst saying, "I would rather be fighting than just waiting."

Gnaeus replied, "It won't be long, something is happening."

Fuscus looked out across towards the fires. Roaring flames clawed at the sky, illuminating the darkness. An orange glow shone across the whole area, which highlighted the massing wolves. He looked back towards his own men. Reviewing and assessing his position. The testudo, still set, was reflecting in the amber light. It moved like a living, breathing creature. Scutums slowly rose and fell, as legionnaires adjusted weary bodies. Fuscus had every confidence they would hold whatever was thrown at them. Behind the rearguard were waiting and ready. Prepared to reinforce immediately.

Fuscus called to them all, "The first has always been the best and the most respected. Men, it has been an utter privilege to serve with you all. I have no doubt that you will make these heathens suffer greatly for their actions." He drew himself up to his full height and shouted, "For honour and for Rome!"

An almighty response echoed: *"For Honour and for Rome."* Titus joined in and followed it with a huge whistle that resonated high into the air.

Lakon lay in the cave entrance, dejected and spiritless, with no desire to move. He lay his head on his front paws, quietly resting. Then he heard a whistle. It was like a bolt of electricity instantly running through his body. He jumped straight up, his ears automatically registering the direction the sound had come from. He looked across, the fires lighting the way towards the sound and legionnaires. His natural ability to see well in the dark let him survey the area effortlessly. He quickly looked from right to left. There was no sign of him. Nothing! As he started to question the sound, Titus lowered his scutum. Lakon's heart raced with excitement. In an instance, he set off. He quietly walked towards the back of the swarming wolves. He plotted a path direct to Titus. With a deep breath, he charged, snarling and growling. Like a demon from the depths of hell, he barrelled through the lines of wolves, knocking over those who didn't move.

Yells and screeches followed his trail. He got to the frontline to find a mass of wolves standing in his way. At full speed, Lakon, a streak of muscle and power, leapt high, hitting the nearest wolf in the centre of his back. The wolf flew forward, hitting a rock hard, as Lakon sailed over his body. He hit the ground, paws pounding, ears flattened against his head. His powerful legs, now at full stretch, cleared the wolves, and he shot across the clearing towards the testudo.

Titus heard the bark! He looked across into the orange gloom to see Lakon charging towards him. He dropped his scutum and dashed forward to meet him. Titus was hit at full tilt, knocking him off his feet. Lakon's joy was explosive. A pure, unfiltered burst of emotion. Wagging furiously, his whole body wriggled with excitement. His bright eyes shone with adoration, jumping, licking, circling. Titus pulled himself up off the ground, laughing and holding Lakon's neck. Cutting the celebration short, Titus heard Sextus' voice saying: "Get back here; they're coming. Bring that big fucker with you, too."

Titus ran back to the group with Lakon close to his heel.

Tarbus walked up to a huge fire. It was stacked high, burning fiercely, as were all the others. He checked the log suspended in the centre, its tip peeled, revealing deep red coals beneath. Tabus smiled. He shouted to Moskon, "Prepare the teams."

Moskon gave the order. Ten wolf teams ran to each fire and picked up the suspended logs. They withdrew the logs, the tips now scorching hot and spitting flames. They spun around, and all ten teams headed to the front of the clearing. They lined up in perfect formation, evenly spaced and aligned with the testudo ranks. The wolf warriors filled in between the gaps and massed behind them. Tarbus and Moskon walked to the front and slowly started to walk forward. The teams and the masses followed suit and gradually picked up pace. From a slow walk, they increased to a slow trot, raising the burning logs to hip height. The tips now flaming, sparking, and spitting, sent a trail of smoke high above the approaching wolves. As they increased pace, the log teams accelerated ahead of the main group. A ten-pointed smoking monster, twenty feet ahead of the rest, careered towards the testudo.

Fuscus called to his men, "Wait for my command. Wait, wait! Testudinem Gyrate."

Gnaeus heard the command and, without hesitation, rotated his scutum. Aulus immediately dropped his scutum, allowing a path to clear. The burning rams, driven by the wolf team, came flying through the now-open gap. The fire and scalding heat from the flaming log burnt and scalded all that it touched. All along the line of its transit, men screamed and cursed but stoically stuck to their duty. Gladius in hand, they stabbed and jabbed at the exposed warriors.

The now hapless ten-headed fire monster, driven by momentum, stumbled through the testudo ranks and was immediately cut down. But for the Romans, it was a brief positional gain. The huge logs in their midst and the wolf bodies now blocked movement. The once fluid process was restricted, and the gaps could not be closed quickly enough. The wolf hordes poured into the testudo through the now gaping holes and charged into the exposed legionnaires.

Titus had positioned himself next to Fuscus with Lakon by his side. A group of wolves came charging in, howling, and falx raised. The first swung high and aimed a powerful blow head height at Titus. It was immediately blocked by his scutum, and a short jab plunged into the overconfident wolf's gut. He screamed and fell at Titus's feet. A second blow from the next wolf was blocked at the last minute. A huge chunk of Titus's scutum, splintering away. Lakon grabbed the warrior's arm and ripped and thrashed until the lacerated arm snapped. Titus drove his blade home, dispatching him.

Sextus was defending hard. His scutum now tattered around the top edge, with huge wield marks across the centre. A pile of dead or squirming wolves was growing around him. An arm wound was pouring with blood. Sextus ignored it with contempt. He stepped forward to block an incoming blow, his precise guard protecting him and exposing the warrior's lunge. A swift push back with his scutum, followed by a straight arm lunge, severed the warriors' intestines.

Fuscus had a broad smile on his face. All his years of command and administration, and yet, at heart, he was a fighting legionnaire. Intelligent, powerful, and quick, he was a force to be reckoned with. Short falx attacks were controlled by speed and strength, his agile footwork putting him in a position to strike. The long falx was kept at range by his scutum, both as a shield and as a weapon. Taking a blow and then ramming the tip up into the nose of the wolf, followed by a slash across the face, his poise and balance were such that he didn't waste any unnecessary energy.

All along the testudo ranks, the scutum walls were falling fast. Individual legionnaires were now battling multiple wolves, the overwhelming numbers now paying dividends. Alulus was desperately defending against two wolves, their falx, slowly chopping his scutum away. As much as he tried, he couldn't gain the upper hand. His years of experience had taught him well, but the falx were deadly and were making the difference. He avoided a low sweep to his legs, which was too close for comfort. The wolf jeered at him and tried the same move. This was Alulus's opportunity. He jumped as the sweep came in and forced his gladius into the wolf's heart. He twisted and withdrew in a fluid motion. Without a moment's pause, another wolf had taken his place. This time, his falx struck, the sweep hitting his left leg, cutting through and breaking the bone. He toppled to the floor, and before he could protect himself, was slashed across the throat by the warrior's second blow.

Gnaeus was in the same situation, surrounded and doing his best to keep them at bay. The larger wolf was armed with a long falx, constantly raining blows into Gnaeus. His scutum was now barely more than a foil, shredded and torn, the centre cross members just holding it together. He had just seen Alulus fall. His lifelong friend, slaughtered. The anger rose in him, and with an almighty yell, he thrust the splintered remains of the scutum straight into the eyes of an incoming wolf.

The blow finally fractured the scutum, and he threw it at another incoming warrior. The wolf knocked it out of the way with his arm and threw his short falx straight into Gnaeus' chest. Gnaeus gasped as the blade penetrated into him. He saw the wolf laugh as the shock and pain hit him. Instinct took over. He lunged straight-armed at the wolf with his gladius. The blade rammed into his groin. With his fading strength, he rotated the blade.

As the wolf screamed in agony, Gnaeus laughed out loud and shouted, "That's your fucking days over."

He dropped to his knees, his head severed by the next incoming warrior.

Tarbus and Mokson had been fighting their way into the remaining Roman forces on the far side of the testudo. Using their fearsome power and swordsmanship, they had driven a wedge halfway through to the back ranks. It had been tough to break the resistance, but slowly, they had broken through. The legionnaires were tiring under the continual onslaught, their scutums disintegrating under the fearful damage inflicted by the falx. A once solid and trusted protection had lost its resistance, splitting under the relentless assault of the enemy blades. Now barely held together, exposing those behind it to the unforgiving wolves.

Tarbus and Mokson withdrew from the spearhead, trusting the following wolves to press forward the advantage they had created. Tarbus surveyed the battlefield. The testudo was fractured all along the front, with wide swathes totally overrun by the wolves. They were gaining the upper hand. However, on the far extreme, the wolves were being held, and many lay dying and injured. In the dim light, he could just make out the white and red plumes of the field commanders. They were at the centre of the carnage. He watched as they engaged their expertly honed skills. Defending with effortless confidence, they probed and pushed for opening opportunities. The counterattack, when it came, was swift and lethal, as a viper's flickering tongue. Flanking them was a legionnaire whose speed and agility surpassed even the officers. Every motion was a masterful display of control. His considered strikes landing before they could be blocked.

As Tarbus studied his movement, the legionnaire surged forward, cutting down an advancing wolf and retreating in one fluid movement. Alongside, the devil dog stayed close, a relentless protector, fending off danger with its unshakable loyalty.

Tarbus called Mokson to follow him. He knew if they could break this stand, they would subdue the resistance and easily overwhelm the rest. They ran along the front of what was the testudo, heading towards the centre of resistance. As they approached, the level of destruction became clearer. Wolves' bodies were strewn in front of the three Romans. The three Romans stayed locked in combat, their actions fluid, their focus unshaken. They had to be stopped, without delay.

Tarbus and Moskon moved forward amongst the battling wolves, positioning themselves to engage the two commanders. Tarbus instructed a group of wolves to pressure the third legionnaire, creating a three-pronged attack. Tarbus finally positioned himself in front of the white plumed commander.

Fuscus saw the huge Dacian leader position himself ready to engage. The power of the man was clear to see. The twin falxes that he wielded were fearsome blades, long yet finally balanced. He gestured to Fucus, taunting and urging him to come forward and engage. Fuscus was far more skilled and seasoned to be drawn. Rather than advance, he positioned himself to absorb the assault he knew was imminent. He awaited the oncoming assault with quiet resolve, steadily preparing his defence. To his left, he saw the other Dacian commander pushing forcefully through the throng of Wolves, positioning himself against Sextus. Though much younger, he was equally powerful in build, evidently the Chief's son.

When the attack came, it surprised Fuscus. For an enormous man, the speed of his feet and balance enabled him to cover the gap between them in seconds. His opening attack brought both falx scissoring either side of Fuscus. It was only the exquisite double-handed defence of scutum and gladius that stopped the first move from seriously wounding Fuscus. The speed and power of the blows battered Fuscus's scutum. A huge chunk snapped off and flew through the air, dropping at the wolf's feet.

Fuscus recovered quickly, pushing the Dacian leader back with a series of sharp stabs forward and a hit to the shoulder with his scutum. The scutum was seriously damaged from all the previous combat. It wasn't the solid platform it had been, and now barely achieved any effect. The wolf laughed and blew on his shoulder to taunt Fuscus.

Recognising the weakness, the wolf started to target the weaker side, powering in long-range falx shots, reducing his risk and decimating the scutum. Fuscus's defense was now almost non-existent, apart from the speed of his gladius. Blocking and striking, he managed to keep just enough distance between himself and the Dacian. Although still fending off the attack, his efforts were tiring him and the gap between the two men was closing fast

Fuscus's options were quickly running out. He tried hard to gain more space, but the wolf kept pressing, raining blows, never appearing to slow or weaken.

Sensing his opportunity, the Dacian feinted a right-handed blow, quickly switching to a left-handed slice. It unbalanced Fuscus, who was still set to defend the non-existent blow. The falx slashed into his right side, slicing clean through the *lorica segmentata*, a testament to the blade's deadly sharpness. The searing pain surged through his body, his right arm now hanging limply at his side. Fuscus reached across with his left arm to boldly grab his gladius for a final defence. The wolf drove down his right hand falx with pure venom, slicing into his exposed shoulder and neck.

Praetorian Prefect Cornelius Fuscus slumped to his knees, gladius still in his hand. He looked up at the huge man in front of him and coughed up a mouth full of blood. Choking, he spat, then smiled and said: "More will come. You have only earned a brief respite." He coughed, then cried out, "For honour and for Rome!" Thrusting forward he presented his neck. The Wolf howled and, with a mighty blow, sliced off his head.

Sextus heard the howl and knew Fuscus had been slain. He closed his eyes and smiled. He remembered the sight of his gallant and slaughtered men. How they had suffered, *all due to the greed and stupidity of Cornelius Fuscus.*

Sextus opened his eyes and saw the huge wolf carving a path through the chaos, aiming straight for him. Like wind through a cornfield, the crowd parted and there he stood before him. A younger man, but his scars told the tale of his experience. Sextus looked to his left across the heaving battle field, and saw the aquilifer still bravely holding the eagle high. The protective legionnaires were still surrounding him, but were dwindling fast. Titus was there, too, furiously battling along with Lakon.

Sextus had fought so many men in his career. As a centurion, his red plumes were always targeted. Time and time again, warriors had come for him. The man to beat and so to destroy the legion's resolve. His arms may ache from the endless blows he had parried, his shield splintered and worn, and his armour scored with deep gashes from those who had tried. Yet, this proud Roman still stood.

He saw the wolf glance at his red-crested helmet. A cruel smile twisted upon the warrior's face. Sextus tightened his grip on his gladius. *Let him come*, he thought. He had faced a hundred like this before.

The barbarian rushed forward, his falx arcing through the air in a savage, overhead strike. Sextus moved with precision, a man who had fought and survived a lifetime of war. He raised his shield at the last moment, angling it so that the blow glanced off. As quick as a heartbeat, a long sweeping left-handed slice came up from the floor, aiming for Sextus's head. It missed, but a triangle of red plumes slowly drifted down to the floor. The wolf tried a stab, followed by another huge slice. Still, Sextus's defense held firm as he watched, measured, and assessed his opponent's every move.

As the wolf poured in the blows, Sextus noticed that he was now slightly hesitating, not quite as fluid. Again, he struck but with less vigour. In a heartbeat of hesitation, Sextus struck. His gladius flashed forward, slicing hard across the top of the wolf's right knee. The warrior staggered, his tendon cut. He swung wildly, his expression betrayed his desperation to land a killing blow. Sextus sidestepped and drove his scutum boss into the man's face. Cartilage crunched, his nose splayed, and his eyes filled with water. Through bleary, blinking eyes, the dacian saw the outline of the gladius before it plunged deep into his heart.

Sextus tore his blade free, lifting it high as he bellowed, "For honour and Rome!"

The Wolves encircling Sextus faltered, stunned as Moskon, son of Tarbus, fell before their eyes. Sextus seized his opportunity. He knocked two wolves out of the way and sprinted across to the eagle. There, beside the aquilifer, and a small group of remaining legionnaires, Sextus, Titus and Lakon made their final stand.

Tarbus hollered with rage. He and the wolves pressed forward, howling. Driven by fury, desperate for revenge. Titus was defending heavily. He had two wolves pressing him, trying to break down his guard. They both tried to press, switched sides, trying to outmanoeuvre him. Each time Titius was exposed, Lakon would be there to defend him. The wolves would pull back from Lakon's attacks, whilst aiming blows at him with their falx. Time and again, they tried. Finally, Titus was able to split the wolves. As one pulled back from a Lakon attack, he stepped too far away. Titus's perfect timing allowed him to step inside. His gladius shot into the side of the first wolf. Pressing the gladius hard into his body, he spun the wolf around and rammed him hard into the second, releasing the blade. A slash across the wolf's throat sent him gagging for breath to the floor.

Tarbus closed in on Titus. The man's hatred showed on his face. They engaged blades flashing under the dim light. Each strike was met with a perfectly timed parry; every opening was ruthlessly closed with expert efficiency. Around them, sharp cries of pain rang out as the relentless wolves cut down the legionnaires protecting the eagle. The unarmed aquilifer, surrounded by warriors, slowly fell to his knees, dying from the many blows he had received. The eagle fell to the floor. An almighty howl filled the air as the eagle was raised, this time in the hands of the Dacian wolves. Ultimately, the sheer numbers had overwhelmed the first cohort.

Titus and Sextus were being pressed backward, defending for their lives. Every block, every parry pushed them closer to the edge of the mountain. Lakon continued to protect Titus where he could, but the falx's now were too many to get close.

Tarbus was driving Titus backward fast. Three wolves were pushing Sextus' defence to its limits. His scutum was all but useless, more for balance than a weapon. He dodged a low stab and chopped an arm in half with a defensive chop.

Side by side, the pair battled. Inch by inch, they cede ground until they could go back no further. Titus faked an attack, and as Tarbus blocked, he was slashed high on his arm. Titus followed up with a short stab that pierced the left arm of Tarbus, making him drop his falx. Titus sensed he was gaining momentum, and the wolf was tiring. He kicked at his knee and saw it buckle, his body weight tipping forward. Titus's gladius shot out and sliced into the now exposed side.

Sextus was still under enormous pressure. His years of experience, the only thing keeping him alive. A wild low swing aimed at his legs came in from the side. Sextus jumped high to avoid the blow. As he landed, he lost his footing on the crumbling surface, toppling backwards. Arms flailing wildly, he struggled to regain his balance. As he tried to steady himself, he slammed bodily into Titus, spinning him round and away from Tarbus.

Gravel skittered beneath their feet, the drop beckoning them downward. Hands grasped at empty air, fingers clawed for anything to halt their fall, without success. No ledge, no outstretched branch. Gravity overtook them, and with a gut-wrenching lurch, the pair plunged over the edge.

Tarbus stood up, his side bleeding, broken but triumphant. He walked over to the destroyed testudo, the bodies of legionnaires strewn throughout. The evidence of their struggle showed in their broken and beaten bodies. Around them lay the masses of dead wolves, who had battled to save their homeland. Tarbus exploded, "Throw those Roman bastards over the edge. They are not fit to lie with our brothers. Their blood will not stain this sacred spot."

Tarbus looked over at Moskon's body, motionless and silent, lying in a pool of blood. It had been a costly price to pay, but he had not failed Decebalus. A thunderous blast from the carnyx tore through the valley, responded to by an almighty howl from Tarbus and the wolves.

Titus lay among the dead and dying, injured and pinned by the sheer weight of the fallen. He heard the tearing, squawking, and constant squabbling. Each ravenous bird fought for the tastiest morsel. Occasionally, a scream would penetrate the air as a bird with a single peck would surgically remove the eyes of a dying warrior. Legionnaires in the prime of health, highly trained, and feared throughout the world, now lay in their thousands. Titus awaited the birds....

CHAPTER 11:
Survival

Venus, the evening star, had climbed far above the horizon. Slowly, it had taken its place in the star-strewn sky. The mass of trees, once lit to a vibrant orange by the firelight, were now just silhouettes against the deepening darkness. The air, thick with the smell of smoke and charred wood, had now cleared, cooling as the night began to settle in.

Tarbus, the warrior chieftain, and the high priest, Vezinas, watched as the thousands of wolf warriors celebrated and howled. Their hoarse voices clashed in a cacophony of noise, with the high-pitched screams of the Draco and the harsh blasts blown from the carnyx. Many warriors had willingly died for their homeland. They had pledged their lives to King Decebalus, vowing to rid their sacred Dacia of the Roman filth that dared to tread upon it. Many thousands of legionnaires now lay dead and dying, ambushed and brutally slain. Their cherished and worshipped eagle standard was now perched on top of a Draco pole, ridiculed by a wolf's skin dangling over its head.

Tarbus turned to Vezinas and said, "The grief for my son and nephew burns in me, yet it is tempered as I know they are now free."

Vezinas replied, "They are with their ancestors and now know what it is to run with the wolves. Tarbus, they eagerly await you when the time is right. Until then, you have your earthly family to protect."

Tarbus walked slowly forward and looked upward at the star-laden sky. A mountain of a man, he was revered by all. A deep sigh left his huge frame, and silent tears started to flow.

His sorrow was broken by a loud blast of horns coming down the Tapae road. A procession of torches, with their flames lighting the trees as they rode downward. As it neared, a huge white stallion came into view. It was surrounded by a guard of six wolf warriors, falx drawn. The four-foot blades of the deadly weapons shimmered as the torchlight flickered and bathed them in a gilded glow.

On top of the stallion rode King Decebalus, the wolf king, protector of the Carpathians, and king of the Dacians. A warrior monarch, broad-shouldered, with a huge dark beard that framed his war-hardened face. His ice-blue eyes projected wisdom, cunning, and resolve.

Not just a ruler but a symbol of Dacian resistance. A strategist of the highest order, a master of deception and ambush. He knew the Dacian terrain like it was part of his own flesh. Using the dense forests, hidden tunnels, and high passes to outwit Rome's machine-like might. Tarbus, still wounded from his combat, slowly moved towards the oncoming procession. He eagerly awaited the arrival of his king and best friend.

Decebalus saw Tarbus limping and struggling to move across to meet him. He promptly spurred his horse forward, surprising his guards as he sped across the clearing towards Tarbus. He reined his horse in roughly and dismounted the stallion in one fluid movement, landing just feet away from Trabus and Vezinas. Decebalus threw open his muscular arms and grabbed his lifelong friend in a warm embrace. Tarbus winced as his still-knitting wounds were crushed open by the man's power.

Decebalus released Tarbus, took a long look into his eyes, and said, "I feel your grief as my own, my friend. Moskon was a son to us both. The gift of his life, along with the other wolf warriors to Dacia, will be celebrated for all time."

Tarbus nodded and replied, "We know our mortal lives are all but a fleeting moment in the eternity of the immortal wolf pack."

Decebalus smiled and instinctively grabbed the gold wolf's head suspended on a leather band around his neck. Decebalus said, "Tarbus, you swore on your life to deliver us from the Roman filth. Your name will be honoured in our history for all time. Stories will be told of Tarbus, Moskon, and your wolves around every campfire forevermore."

Tarbus flashed a broad grin, his eyes gleaming with pride. Vezinas vigorously shook the Draco pole, and the wolf skin on top, covering the eagle standard, swayed precariously.

Decebalus continued, " Come, drink with me; tell me all. I want to hear what you have learnt. How well our plans unfolded. How the Roman filth screamed when they were hit by the logs. How Fuscus grovelled and pleaded for his life."

The three men turned and walked towards the last remaining fire. Laughing and exchanging stories, their voices rose loudly in the crisp night air.

As the early morning mist settled around him, Lakon, crawled out from the thick bush. He had lain silently all night under its gnarled and twisted branches, quietly hidden from the rampaging warriors. The wind had sighed as though the trees themselves were whispering warnings. Every crack and groan was a reminder of the danger that awaited above.

In the last minutes of the final attack on Titus and Sextus, he had desperately been trying to protect them both. Grabbing at arms and legs, biting, and ripping whilst avoiding the deadly swinging falx. He had frantically leapt at an attacker getting too close to Titus. In mid-air, he was hit on the chest by a club, knocking him down over the edge, sprawling into the thorn bush. As he gathered his senses and scrambled to free himself, he saw Centurion Sextus above him fighting on the ridge. Sextus jumped to avoid a low falx blow aimed at his legs. He stumbled, lost his footing, and then barrelled into Titus. He had seen his master Titus spiral over the edge scrabbling with his hands, grabbing at the vegetation to try and stop his fall. Sextus's added weight had increased his momentum, and in a moment, the pair were tumbling over the ledge.

Lakon had heard the wolf warriors' howls and shouts of celebration. The sound of the Draco and carnyx, screeching and rasping coarsely through the night air. He had also heard the screams of the wounded legionnaires as they and their dead comrades were hurled over the edge. Downward, they plunged, dropping onto the bodies of the Romans who had been swept over by the avalanche of logs.

Lakon still sensed the extreme danger that lurked above. He reviewed his surroundings. Peering through the mist, he saw that the slope back up to the clearing was far too steep for him to climb. Below him, thick bushes clung to the shale-laden ground. Their roots plunged deep, anchoring them firmly on the steep slope leading to the edge. Through the gloom, almost halfway down, he could just make out what looked like a very narrow goat track. The slope was treacherous, offering a natural refuge from humans and enabling animals to traverse the mountain with ease.

Lakon carefully turned around and started the steep descent. His paws slid and slipped under his massive bulk. Skidding and scrambling in the shale, he tried to keep his balance and control his descent. As his speed increased, flints dug into the flesh of his paws, ripping and tearing, making it harder to contain his pace. Summoning every shred of his power, he pushed down with all his might, resisting gravity as it pulled him towards the beckoning edge. As he reached the track, he swung his huge body sharply to the right, immediately dropping to the floor and anchoring himself safely. A colossal stream of shale, dust and dirt flew past him. Surging onward, it plunged forward and poured down over the ledge.

Lakon lay totally still, catching his breath. Silently, he listened for any sounds coming from above. Had any of the warriors heard the shale fall and become curious? All he could hear were the distance howls and the remaining dirt sliding past him. Quietly, he got to his feet and started along the twisting track.

Cautiously, he walked through the thick mist. The cool, damp air pressed against his skin. Each breath he took was a sharp chill that, when released, billowed in the air like a wisp of smoke before vanishing back into the mist. Ghostly fingers from branches of trees and bushes gradually appeared, penetrating the heavy veil that blurred the world beyond. He could now see the mangled and broken legionnaires' bodies that had been swept from the Tapae road. The evidence of the brutal slaughter and devastation caused by the log ambush now hung from branches or lay strewn and crumpled. Some in piles stopped by the dense thickets, other individual bodies, their ghostly fear-stricken features frozen, lay along the path.

Lakon was driven forward by some unknown force. His olfactory senses drew him onward, ignoring the horror that was slowly being exposed. He knew that he had to keep moving. The path twisted steeply downward, edging ever closer towards the sheer drop. Carefully, he manoeuvred his great bulk down, skidding to a stop at the bottom. There, he was confronted by a large pile of legionnaires' bodies, balancing precariously and blocking his way forward. There was no way around. He either had to retrace his steps back or find a way to move ahead. Lakon had no fear of the dead; he had fought in many battles alongside Titus. He carefully climbed up on top of the bodies and looked ahead. The small path created by mountain goats had collapsed, creating a seven-foot gap between Lakon and the path that continued ahead. He stood and sniffed the air. Again, an unknown force beckoned him forward.

Lakon turned and climbed down the pile of bodies. He walked back a further ten feet to the end of the path just before it turned upward sharply. Coiling his powerful body, he dug his hind legs into the path and sprang forward. As he gained top speed, he reached the pile of bodies. Digging hard with his enormous shoulders and front legs, he powered up to the top of the pile. With inches to spare, he launched himself, sailing over the gap. Lakon could see the opposite side looming up fast, but his speed was dropping. He extended his body as far as he could, his front legs outstretched, claws extended. The wind whistled violently through his ears as he came down hard, hitting the side of the collapsed path. He wildly dug his front paws into the top of the path but instantly could feel himself starting to slip backwards. Gradually, hard as he tried, he lost his grip. His giant back legs scrambled in mid-air, looking for some form of support. His efforts were in vain and resulted in creating even greater downward momentum. Lakon tried with all of his might, but his massive bulk was now acting against him. He was now inches from falling.

Two powerful hands grabbed Lakon's chain link collar. These were followed by two further hands that cupped under his front legs.

"Hang onto the big bastard!" shouted Lucius.

"He weighs a fucking tonne., Pull!" shouted Quintus.

Together, the brothers edged backwards, dragging the mighty dog with them. Lakon felt his back legs touch something firm, and he pushed with all his strength. He and the two men went sprawling, just stopping themselves from spilling back over the side.

Quintus stood up, his recently acquired wolf skin covered in dust. He looked at Lakon and then turned to his brother, saying, "I told you it was Titus's dog. I would know this monster anywhere."

Lucius replied, "What has happened to Titus? The dog would never be separated from him. It's obvious he was determined to reach someone or somewhere by attempting such a crazy jump."

Lakon sniffed Quintus. He knew his scent. He had met him previously in the forest with Titus and was not a threat. He rammed his giant head against Qunitus's leg, turned, walked a few steps, and then stopped, looking back at Quintus. His eyes were blazing bright. Their intensity seemed to sear into Quintus's consciousness.

"He wants us to follow him," said Quintus. "Lucius," he added, "grab the packs. We have to go with him."

The two brothers, Quintus and Lucius, were chief scouts from Legio V Alaudae. They had escaped the ambush and slaughter purely by luck. On escaping the cart they had been tied to, they knew they had no chance of fighting the Dacian onslaught alone. Both had silently slid down the steep slope, heading away from the rampaging wolf warriors. Halfway down, they had discovered the goat track running along the mountainside. They stealthily made their way along the path, keeping out of sight as much as possible. They could see the path ran parallel to the Tapae road, towards where the overnight stronghold might have been built. It would have been the only possibility to provide safety for at least the first and second cohorts. As they made their way along the twisting path, the brothers discovered the mass slaughter and horror caused by the Dacian ambush. They had heard the howling of the wolf warriors, the blasts of carnyx, and the screaming of their colleagues as they were massacred and slain.

As night drew in, what appeared to be a torch flickering came into view. Its light was illuminating the entrance to a cave set back in the sandstone. They listened for any noise, and when they were sure it was safe, they entered, finding supplies of food, water, and weapons. Clearly a supply store for the wolf warriors. Taking the torch, they explored further. At the back of the cave, there was a series of tunnels appearing to lead deeper into the mountainside. Stairs had been meticulously chiselled. Some headed upward, whilst others appeared to be going steeply down.

Whilst Quintus kept guard, Lucius carefully descended some of the way down. As he turned a corner, he could see far below that the stairs continued downwards. Moonlight shone in and clearly bathed the steps. He resisted the urge to go deeper and climbed back up the stairs. As he ascended, he discovered a carved ledge set back from the stairwell. It was wide enough for a man to sleep and was covered with a small pile of wolf skins. Lucius grabbed two of the skins and swiftly returned to Quintus.

They returned the torch to its stone holder by the door, ensuring that its light would not be missed. Both men pulled the wolf skins over their tunics and set out to search for some safety. Deep in the cave, hidden in the darkness, they nervously awaited the morning light.

As dawn broke, they carefully continued along the path. The brothers hoped the early morning mist would act as a thin veil, distorting their wolf warrior disguises and providing them with some safety. Quintus heard a noise and saw a momentary flash of black ahead. It sounded like something was sliding down the steep shale embankment. He silently grabbed Lucius' shoulder and pulled him to the ground. He put his fingers to his lips and pointed forward. Ahead, a huge pile of stricken legionnaires were teetering on the edge of the mountainside. Quintus could see that in front of them, the path had collapsed, creating a huge rift.

As both men watched, a huge dog appeared on top of the bodies. It stood still and sniffed the air. They saw the distinct Roman chain collar around its neck. Only one Roman war dog matched that size; it could only be Lakon, Titus's monster. The dog turned around and again disappeared. Within seconds, they saw it charging up over the pile of bodies and, with a final great bound, leapt full length across the rift. Quintus watched as the dog appeared to be flying. Its ears were pressed behind its head, with the jet-black body totally horizontal. It seemed that the valiant effort was going to work.

At the last minute, his speed dropped, and Lakon crashed heavily, landing short and hitting the side of the path. The enormous animal was now clinging on for its life. Slowly, its two front paws, claws fully extended, were sliding backwards. Lakon whined in fear. Deep grooves appeared in the loose dirt, now only inches from the drop. The brothers sprinted along the path. They grabbed its collar to stop the initial slide backwards. Then, by supporting its weight, Lakon gained a foothold, and his incredible strength pushed all three backwards, with the brothers landing in a pile.

Lakon set off at pace. Quintus and Lucius did their best to keep up, the narrow and treacherous path continually slowing their efforts. Lakon was acting on instinct, seemingly without conscious thought. Occasionally stopping, his mighty head sniffed the air and then set off with renewed purpose.

As the sun rose, its warmth slowly banished the thick mist that had settled over the valley. The dense curtain of fog began to part, revealing the hidden landscape beneath. Quintus and Lucius stopped in their tracks. A scene of total horror unfolded before their eyes. Thousands of Roman legionnaires, in grotesque piles, had been driven to their deaths by the avalanche of Dacian logs. Broken bodies lay strewn across the valley floor. Splintered logs had pierced multiple legionnaires whilst marching in formation. Ripping through their torsos with brutal force, the impact sent them tumbling helplessly, bodies spinning uncontrollably as they plummeted to their deaths. Many had been brutally struck by the logs, the force propelling them into the air and over the edge. Some had been speared by the branches of the many trees lining the mountainside. Others collided with the jagged rocks below, their rough, weathered surfaces jutting out from the slow-moving river. Those who had survived the fall were now trapped beneath the dark, suffocating water. Their shattered, motionless bodies were unable to escape the crushing weight of their armour.

Quintus and Lucius had fought in countless brutal campaigns. Battle-hardened by unrelenting violence, they had witnessed horrors to haunt even the bravest. Yet this unspeakable nightmare shattered them, pushing their resolve to breaking point. Overcome, they sank to their knees, their strength drained, whilst tears flowed freely.

Lakon was ahead of the brothers but sensed their emotions. He stopped and quietly walked back to stand silently by the men. The three looked out over the valley and the horrifying scene. A murder of large black Carrion crows now flew over the bodies. One by one, they dropped out of the sky and started to feast on the festering limbs and torsos. Their excited cries tore through the deathly silence, shattering the stillness that hung over the valley.

Lakon's growl jolted the brothers from their desolation. He pushed his weight against Lucius and once again set off up the path. Quintus and Lucius picked up their packs and weapons, sprinting to catch up with Lakon, who again was surging forward.

As the brothers turned a sharp bend in the path, they saw Lakon sitting a hundred yards ahead, waiting for them. They instantly recognised it was the cave entrance. As they grew nearer, they could see the entry torch had recently burnt out. Thin wisps of black smoke gently spiralled upward, instantly dissolving in the morning air.

Lakon entered the cave without hesitation. He moved straight toward the carved stairs, paused for a moment, looked at the brothers, and then began descending the steep spiral stairwell. Quintus turned to Lucius and joked, "If that big bastard is happy to go down there, I'd rather be with him than up here alone with you!"

Before Lucius could reply, Quintus set off, heading into the darkness. The spiral stairs were a twisted, grim passage of weathered stone, their edges worn smooth by the passage of countless wolf warrior feet. The walls seemed to close in, casting shadows that swallowed the last of the natural light. Lakon had pushed ahead, senses alive to his surroundings, he detected no danger. The faint echo of his scuttling footsteps hung in the air, adding to the eerie, timeless feeling of the shaft.

Quintus and Lucius carefully negotiated the dark, steep stairs. Hands on the sidewalls, they inched their way down, seeking any stability they could find as they descended further into the unknown. The steepness of the stairs and the rounded edges of the steps further contributed to the danger of their descent, leaving no room for error. The darkness pressed in around them, their eyes desperately searching for any tiny relief of light that could provide some comfort. The deeper they went, the darkness and sense of the unknown amplified their unease, constantly gnawing at their raw nerves. Still, they heard the echoes of Lakon's scuttling footsteps, an element of comfort in the inky void.

The brothers reached a sharp turn in the shaft, where the gloom swallowed everything beyond their reach. As their eyes adjusted, it appeared as though the stairs dropped away into a jet-black abyss. Cautiously, Quintus moved forward. Lucius followed, his hands resting on the shoulders of his brother in front, ready to pull him back. Together, they navigated the steep, tight, winding bend, their movements slow and deliberate., As they finally negotiated the right-angled bend, a thin shaft of light pierced the darkness from below. Lucius thought back to the previous night and the faint glow of moonlight he had seen. As miniscule as it was, it penetrated through the shadows, providing a welcoming illumination of the narrow passage ahead. As they again became accustomed to the light, they could see Lakon sitting, waiting patiently at the end of the passage.

He growled, looked hard at Quintus, walked slowly down the passage, and was instantly out of sight. They quickly followed, and as they turned the right-angled bend, they saw a hundred feet ahead. Lakon sat by a door with light streaming around its frame. Their hearts lept. The brilliant light provided them with a welcoming beacon of hope, yet still, ominous fear. Promising both escape from the tunnel and yet, the ever presence of danger. Quintus and Lucius exchanged uneasy glances, and their thoughts flickered back to what they knew the valley held outside.

Lakon clawed at the door with all his might. His blow sent a resounding shock wave up through the passageway. Continually echoing, it repeated and carried onward and up the stone stairwell. Quintus moved toward the door. He saw that it was secured by a large stone slab, just leaning against the door. A simple but effective way that would require considerable strength to push it back from the outside. He bent down to the slab, lifted it upright, and rolled it away from the door.

Lakon excitedly jumped alongside Quintus, his eyes shining and tail wagging urgently. Lucius picked up their packs and weapons and stood ready. Quintus grabbed the door, gave a heave, and it opened wide.

CHAPTER 12

Sixth Sense

Titus lay among the dead and dying, injured and pinned by the sheer weight of the fallen. All around him, he could hear the tearing, squawking, and constant squabbling as each ravenous carrion crow fought for the tastiest morsel. Occasionally, a scream would penetrate the air as a bird, with a single peck, would surgically remove the eye of a dying warrior. Legionnaires in the prime of health, highly trained, and feared throughout the world now lay in their thousands.

The sound of the birds grew ever closer. He could hear the clicks of their sharp beaks as they pecked and snapped at the bodies around him. Try as he might to move, the weight of the dead piled on his lower legs held him fast. Hours ago, the numbness and tingling had started in his legs. Every effort to free himself now caused him excruciating pain. Desperately, he fought the urge to scream, terrified that the wolf warriors would learn he was still alive.

Titus remembered the initial fall clearly, the weight of Sextus hitting him and knocking him off balance. Scrabbling and grabbing at vegetation, they tried to slow their descent as they careered towards the edge. The feeling of weightlessness as they left the mountainside, followed by the sudden drop as gravity once again won its constant battle. Sextus, the heavier man of the two, plunged downward, bouncing through the canopies of the huge trees. His body hit a large branch and went cartwheeling through the lower branches, finally slumping amongst the dead.

Titus was more fortunate. His scutum had caught around his gladius scabbard and now acted as a brake. As he plunged downward, the scutum hit the tree branches, reducing the momentum of his fall. He bounced through the heavily leafed branches, gradually slowing. As he fell, Titus hit his head on a branch with a sickening thud; instantly, darkness engulfed him. The scutum broke free, dropped, and finally speared the ground, wedging vertically between the legs of a dead legionnaire. Titus's limp body broke through the last branches and landed beside the upright, wedged scutum.

Titus awoke the blackness slowly lifted as his consciousness returned. Pain surged through his body, and he realised his feet and ankles were pinned beneath a pile of the dead. Titus looked down at his legs and saw that his life had been spared by the stoic scutum. The crushing weight of legionnaires' bodies, hurled over by the wolf warriors, now rested atop the shield, teetering above his torso.

Broken bodies, twisted and bloated, were already beginning to putrefy. Flesh turning pale, their swollen eyes now dull and vacant. The all-encompassing stench of death enveloped him. Mangled flesh, congealing blood, merged with evacuated bowels, all clung to the back of his gasping, parched throat. Each breath burnt his lungs, causing him to gag and retch. There was no escaping it. Not here, not in this valley of horror, where death had sown its deadly seed.

Quintus opened the door wide with a huge tug. Bright sunlight blazed into his eyes, causing him to stumble back, momentarily blinded. As his vision adjusted to the glare, the scene of desolation he had glimpsed from the mountainside fully revealed its horrific consequences. The Dacian ambush had been devastatingly effective, total in its execution. Never before had he witnessed such punishment inflicted upon the elite of the Roman Empire.

Lucius stepped through the doorway and stood alongside Quintus. He could see his brother trembling. He looked along the valley at the hordes of legionnaires. Once a force to be feared, now just a mass of corpses.

How could Praetorian Prefect Cornelius Fuscus have been so naive? he thought. His lust for the Dacian gold and personal glory had caused the destruction of all these men.

He remembered the sight of the legions marching in formation along the Tapae road. Proud and resolute, the eagle standard glinted in the sun, the zenith of Roman might. His thoughts were broken by loud squawking and screeching. Two huge carrion crows fought each other over the remains of a freshly plucked eyeball. The grizzly remains now dripped from each of the bird's beaks.

Lakon barged the brothers apart, his huge mass easily pushing them out of his way. Once again, his senses were leading him, and he set off at pace towards the bodies.

"Quick, follow him," said Quintus. "He must have picked up on a scent."

Lucius grabbed Quintus by his shoulder, held him fast, and said, "What if we are seen in the open valley? The wolf warriors will come for us?"

Quintus looked at his brother, slowly shook his head, and then said, "Lucius, we are already living on borrowed time. By the will of the gods, our lives were spared. There must have been a reason. I believe we only have one course of action, and it is to follow Lakon, whatever the risks to ourselves."

Lucius looked up to the sky. The sun, partially veiled by towering white clouds, cast sparkling rays of light that beamed out from behind them. Yet its gentle warmth still caressed Lucius. He felt a surge of hope rise within him. They had survived for a reason. He turned to Quintus, smiled, and said, "You are right. We have made it this far. We have to follow Lakon."

The brothers collected their belongings and chased after Lakon. They could see the great beast purposefully moving between the piles of bodies, his tail wagging furiously as he followed his senses. With each group he approached, he would pause, sniff, process, and then move on with renewed vigour. Lakon's pace was growing quicker, a silent intensity now driving him forward.

Titus was struggling to maintain consciousness. His body was trembling with pain, and his brain craved relief. He hadn't drunk any water since the start of the battle. Now, his raging thirst was restricting his throat and making it hard for him to breathe.

As hard as he tried to resist, hallucinations were occurring more regularly and becoming more surreal. Apparitions flooded his mind, teasing and tormenting him. His mother appeared, beckoning him to her, smiling, with her hand outstretched. "Titus," she whispered, "come to me. Let me take your pain away. You know I love you, and you will always be safe in my hands."

His mother wistfully looked over her shoulder and his father then came into view, walking down through the olive groves. The old farm buildings he remembered fondly were shining white in the bright Spanish sunshine. Holding out the reins of his favourite pony, his father called to him, "Come, Titus. You and I will ride into the forest and hunt the wild boar together. We shall light a fire and cook a meal for the family."

Titus eagerly raised his hand to grab the reins, and in a moment, they vanished into thin air.

Once again, he saw his mother, but now, she was much younger with long jet black hair that hung loosely down her back. She was in a forest clearing, cooking on an open fire, surrounded by trees, their trunks soaring upward to a canopy of sun-kissed foliage. Sat at her feet was a small dark-haired boy, playing happily with a pair of golden wolves. The boy ignored Titus for a short while and then stopped his game, looked directly up at him, and smiled. Purposefully, he raised his right arm, a golden wolf held tightly in his closed hand. Slowly, he opened his hand and offered the gleaming gold wolf upward.

Titus heard himself speak to the boy in a language he knew from the distant past, "No, you must keep both Lakon & Zibel. They must run together forever."

The boy nodded solemnly whilst a faint smile flickered across his face. He turned to his mother, showing her he had kept both his wolves. His mother smiled lovingly at Titus and whispered, "Valez duanai. Be safe on your journey."

Then, both the boy and his mother slowly faded from sight, leaving Titus overwhelmed by a profound sense of loss and sorrow.

Titus fought with all his strength to resist lapsing back into the welcoming twilight world. Increasingly, it embraced him, ever more enticing him to succumb. He shook his head, fighting every spasm and wave of pain that spread through his body.

Again, he felt himself drift into his world of dreams. Lakon, his faithful companion, now bounded up to him, his huge face beaming with joy. His wet tongue licked his face whilst his giant paws pulled and dug around his shoulders. Titus tried to speak to him, but no sound would come from his throat. His chest rose as he struggled for air whilst tears of frustration streamed from his eyes and ran down his cheeks.

Quintus saw Lakon stop and sniff the air, and then his whole body stiffened. In one bound, the huge beast jumped towards a pile of bodies that were balanced on the top of an upright scutum. The sheer weight of the bodies was now pressing downward, causing the shield to bow in the middle, ready to fracture. The dog drove his head down and appeared to be licking vigorously. He then started to dig, his massive front paws driving forward. Quintus ran over to Lakon and, to his amazement, saw Titus's body lying prostrate. Lucius arrived and knelt down beside Titus. He put his hand on his chest and was amazed to find Titus was still breathing. Faint breath, unconscious, yet alive.

Lakon sat and watched intensely as Lucius tried to revive Titus. He carefully dropped small drops of water onto his lips, trying not to choke him with a sudden rush of water down into his throat. Titus's tongue slowly appeared through his blistered lips, exploring the sensation of moisture. Gradually, Lucius increased the flow as Titus's breathing increased.

Quintus was carefully inspecting the pile of bodies, propped up by the scutum, which threatened to break under the immense weight. He was concerned that if Titus regained consciousness, he might wave his arms around in shock. One solid hit to the fractured shield and the whole pile would descend down onto him. He quickly collected a leather strap from his bag, pushed one end under Titus's body, and securely tied his arms against his side.

Lucius was increasing the volume of water when Titus gave a mighty cough and spat out a wedge of dust and phlegm. His eyes opened wide, and he looked directly into Lucius's face. He saw the wolf skin, and instantly, a look of terror spread across his face. Titus tried to move his arms in defence, but as much as he struggled, they were held fast.

Lucius recognised his fear and quickly pulled the wolf skin backwards, revealing his full features.

Titus exhaled, his voice rasp. "I thought my time had come. How long have I been here?"

Before Lucius could answer, Lakon barged forward and gently growled, followed by a flurry of licks drenching Titus's face.

Quintus spoke to Lucius, "We have to move these bodies quickly. The whole thing is going to collapse at any moment ."

As if to prove his point, the scutum gave a crack and sagged slightly. The brothers sprang to their feet and, after taking positions on either side of the pile, began the gruesome task of peeling away each dead legionnaire's body. Each one was interlocked in some way with another. Rigor mortis locked bodies together, twisting them into a grotesque embrace. They worked carefully, untangling the corpses when possible.

Though often, they were forced to snap rigid limbs to release those who were interlocked.

As they manhandled the last corpse free, the indomitable scutum gave a mighty crack, finally snapping. Quintus and Lucius were left holding the body suspended in the air as the separate pieces of the scutum fell broken onto Titus's chest. Respectfully, they placed the last body onto the ground. At last, the reason became clear why Titus couldn't move. Two fully armoured legionnaire corpses were laid across Titus's feet and ankles, pinning him down.

Titus was now fully conscious and demanding more water. Quintus freed the rope from his arms and gave Titus the gourd to drink from. He took a long gulp, coughed again, and said to Quintus, "I can't feel my feet or ankles. They are numb. Have they been severed?"

"No," Quintus said. "They are trapped, and the circulation to them has been completely cut off. When we move the weight, and it returns, it is going to be bad. Titus, prepare yourself."

Titus could see the brothers move down to the first body. They tried to move it, but it wouldn't move. They once again took it by the legs and, with a huge tug, pulled it free. A slight tingle of sensation crept up Titus's right leg as the weight reduced.

Lucius turned to Titus and said, "Are you ready?"

Titus nodded and waited. Quintus had the second body by its arms and pulled it clear from Titus, freeing his legs completely.

At first, it was only numbness. A quiet, crawling numbness, inch by inch, within his bones. The tips of his toes, up through his feet to his ankles, ascended up to his calf muscles. The pressure of the weight now released freed the restricted flow of Titus's blood. Once a struggling trickle, it turned into a raging river. Pulsing through arteries and veins, reawakening starved nerves.

Titus felt as if his legs were ablaze, white-hot fire racing through frozen muscle. Every cell shrieked as oxygen flooded back. His muscles twitched and seized in uncontrollable, violent, cramping spasms. He thrashed involuntarily, sweat pouring, fighting the desire to scream out loud. His hands grabbed the edges of his lorica segmentata, squeezing as hard as he could to resist the scorching pain coursing through his limbs. As he reached the limit of his control, there was one final spasm, and with a huge gasp of relief, the pain began to subside.

Slowly, he twisted his ankles, rotating them to reduce the numbness. Regaining control of his feet and ankles, he gradually raised his legs. At last, he could draw his knees upwards and, with some effort, swung them around so he was sitting upright. The rush of movement sent his head reeling, and he would have fallen backwards had Lakon's great bulk not held him steady.

Quintus looked at Lakon and then turned to Titus, saying, "You owe your life to that beast of yours. He somehow knew where you had fallen. He led us straight to you."

Lucius pointed up towards the battle site far up in the distance. "Right from up there," he said.

Titus grabbed Lakon's great head and shoulders, hugged him, and slapped his back hard. Quintus reached into his bag and pulled out some dried meat they had found in the Dacian cave. He gave Titus and Lakon a chunk each. Both man and dog hungrily devoured the offering.

The three men sat silently, contemplating the devastating scene around them. It was Lucius that broke the silence. "Titus," he said, "the whole campaign has been decimated. There may be some other possible survivors, but I fear not. Quintus and I moved up from the rear of the column, slipping along a hidden goat track and staying out of the wolf warriors' sight. The Dacian ambush and attack devastated each legion. We saw bodies strewn all along the road. Others plunged to their deaths, hit by the logs or, like yourself, were thrown or fell. This valley is a mass graveyard for so many elite legions of Rome."

Quintus asked, "Titus, do you feel you are able to walk? The wolf warriors will soon be down here in the valley, looting the bodies. Our only chance is to make our way back to the Castra and then cross the Danube. We must report."

Lucius joined in, "Nightfall is only hours away. The quicker we can get out of the valley and move towards the fort, the greater our chance to survive."

Titus put his hand on Lakon's head, stroked down his back, and thought back to his meeting with Corneilus Fuscus. He remembered their conversation and could visualise the wooden wax tablet that contained his direct orders from Emperor Domitian: "Find the gold. Infiltrate Decebalus's fortress and discover his weaknesses." He took a moment to ponder his situation. It was a direct order from the emperor! Yet what Quintus was saying made total sense. This affront to the Roman Empire had to be reported. A major force must be raised to seek retribution and eradicate the Dacian nation.

Titus slowly stood, using Quintus's shoulders for support. His eyes scanned the fallen, and he spotted a gladius lying on the ground. Carefully, he shuffled toward the weapon, willing his feet and ankles to obey.

He bent down, inspected the blade, and, with a practised motion, slid it into his empty scabbard. "Quintus, you are right," said Titus. "This heinous act must be repaid twofold. Emperor Domitian will view this as a direct threat to his power and authority. He will not let it be perceived as a weakness of the empire. We have to make it our mission to report back."

Quintus and Lucius smiled and nodded in agreement. They got to their feet, collected their packs, and readied themselves. Lucius led the way, turning towards the end of the valley and the safety of the Danube. He had only gone four steps when a hand grabbed his leg with iron force, stopping him in his tracks. Lucius yelled.

A low voice growled, "Where are you pair of fuckers going without me?"

Lucius went white as a sheet, his whole body shaking uncontrollably.

The voice continued, "Now get me out from under these poor bastards."

Titus shouted, "Sextus, you are alive!"

Quintus and Titus moved closer and took stock of Sextus's predicament.

Titus asked: "Sextus, how did you survive? What injuries do you have?"

Sextus replied less aggressively, "My arm is broken, as well as my right leg. I don't know how I survived. I only remember flying past you through the trees and hitting the branch. I woke up trapped and couldn't move these two off of me."

Quintus shook Lucius and said, "Get to the other side and grab the legs."

Lucius duly walked around to behind Sextus and picked up the legs of the huge legionnaire. Quintus bent down and took hold of the man's arms.

"Right," said Quintus, "let's see if we can drag him gently over to the right. Take care not to catch him on the other body below."

The two men heaved, and slowly, the giant man, inch by inch, was dragged over and away from Sextus. They dropped his great bulk with a sigh of relief. Sextus groaned with the shift in weight as his broken leg flexed. The two brothers returned to the remaining body, a much smaller man.

Quintus said to Sextus, "Get ready; this is going to hurt."

Sextus growled: "Get on with it, man."

Quintus looked across at Titus standing with Lakon. Titus briefly grinned and nodded. Quintus took hold of the legs whilst Lucius grabbed the shoulders.

Carefully as possible, they lifted straight upwards, releasing the whole weight from Sextus's body.

Sextus Aemilius, Centurion Primus Pilus of the First Cohort, Legio V Alaudae, flinched silently in great pain. A man hardened by years of battle, who would never, could never, display any weakness. He led from the front; his men admired and feared him in equal measure.

Titus spoke quietly to Sextus, "We have to move you. The wolf warriors will be coming soon. We must head towards the Danube."

Sextus nodded, clearly in pain. "Do it," he said.

Quintus interrupted: "How are we going to move him? He won't be able to walk with his injuries. It will slow us down!"

Titus inhaled deeply, turning over the gravity of the situation. He looked over at Sextus, still lying on the ground, his face ashen, battling the pain. Behind him sat Lakon, ever alert, listening and guarding. He always marvelled at the sheer size and power the dog possessed. Ferocious in battle, unwavering in loyalty

As he considered their problem, he saw two unbroken scutums lying on top of two bodies. Titus looked at Sextus, looked back at the scutum and then again over at Lakon. A gem of an idea sprung into his mind. He quickly walked over to the brothers and said,

"We will make a sledge to carry Sextus. Get those two scutums and tie them together lengthwise."

Lucius spoke up, "So, are we going to pull him?"

"No," said Titus. He looked across to Lakon and replied, "Lakon will."

Quintus thought for a moment and then smiled, saying, "It just might work. I'll create a harness from the rope and scavenged straps from the bodies. Lucius, you fashion a sledge from the two scutums."

Titus said, "I will create some splints for Sextus's arm and leg. Hopefully, it will ease the pain as he bounces along."

The three set off to their chosen tasks, and within an hour, they were ready to test the sledge. Titus had fashioned two splints from parts of broken scutum and used strips from tunics to secure them in place. He organised the brothers around Sextus. He took hold of Sextus' leg and gently raised it. Sextus was sweating profusely. His fists were tightly clenched, yet not a single murmur left his mouth. With the brothers supporting the leg, he placed a splint on either side so that they extended beyond the break, stabilising the bone. He stuffed strips of cloth between them and then tied further strips around the leg, securing the splint in place. Titus nodded and they gently lowered the leg.

Sextus wiped his brow and said, "Get the fucking arm done now."

Once completed, the three men surrounded Sextus. Carefully, they lifted him over to the scutum-built sledge, laying him gently down. Titus took the securing straps and tied them tightly around Sextus's body. The harness Lucius had made was fitted onto Lakon, and he was then led to the front of the sledge. Titus knelt down and stroked Lakon's head. The dog looked at him and turned his head to the side, almost knowingly understanding his challenge ahead. Titus stood up and connected the harness to the sledge ropes. He walked all the way around it, carefully checking that the ropes and knots were secure. When he was satisfied, he said to all three, "Are we ready?"

Neither spoke. Quintus and Lucius just nodded their agreement. The decision had been made. Sextus stirred. His eyes, closed tight against the pain, opened slowly. He shifted his head, wincing as he turned towards the three figures looming above him. His voice, rough and low, growled, "Thank You. Now let's fuck off out of this hell hole."

To be continued...

COLIN DEAN

DRACO RETURN

PART TWO:
FIRST BATTLE OF
TAPAE

Following the devastating slaughter of the Roman legions, Emperor Domitian found himself humiliated and desperate to restore his honour. To reclaim Rome's pride, he dispatches the seasoned senator and general, Tettius Julianus, with a single mission: crush King Decebalus and bring Dacia to its knees.

In Draco Return, our heroes are vital to the success of this bold campaign. Can they aid Julianus in defeating Decebalus and recovering the lost legionary standard? Will they uncover the elusive treasure that lured Cornelius Fuscus into a fatal trap, one that led to the slaughter of thousands of his men?

To be continued....

FOOTNOTE FACTS

1: Cornelius Fuscus Campaign Trail

The terrain encountered by Cornelius Fuscus during his campaign in Dacia was highly challenging.

Key features included:

Mountainous Terrain:

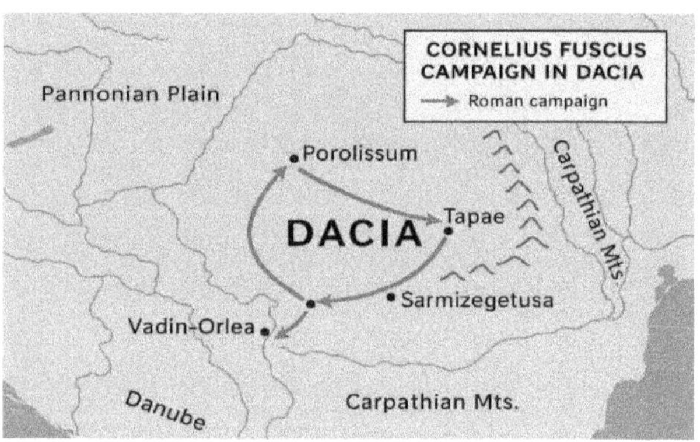

The Carpathian Mountains formed a significant natural barrier that the Roman forces had to navigate. These mountains were steep, rugged, and dense with forests, creating difficulties for both supply lines and large-scale troop movements. The high altitude also made it harder to sustain an army, particularly with limited routes through the mountains.

Dense Forests:

The area was heavily wooded, particularly in the regions around Sarmizegetusa and the Carpathians. These forests provided excellent cover for Dacian ambushes and made it difficult for Roman soldiers to maintain effective formations, especially for the larger Roman legions. The dense cover also made communication and supply lines vulnerable.

Rivers and Swamps:

The Danube River was a natural boundary and provided a major crossing point for Roman forces. The river itself was vital for the transport of men and supplies, but crossing it posed logistical and strategic challenges. The Tisza River also flowed through the region, and its surrounding marshes added to the difficulty of manoeuvring.

In some areas, swampy terrain further complicated movement and could slow down Roman progress.

Dacian Fortifications:

The Dacians had well-fortified strongholds, most notably the fortress at Sarmizegetusa, which was located on an elevated plateau and protected by steep cliffs. These fortifications were difficult to breach and heavily fortified, requiring significant Roman effort to overcome.

Hostile Forces:

Dacian forces, led by King Decebalus, were highly familiar with the local terrain, giving them a strategic advantage in ambushes and defensive operations. Dacians were skilled in guerrilla tactics and took full advantage of their knowledge of the forests and mountain passes, making it difficult for the Romans to maintain control over key areas.

All these factors, combined with the poor decision making of Fuscus made the campaign much harder than anticipated and led to the losses they sustained.

2: *Cornelius Fuscus Praetorian Prefect*

Cornelius Fuscus was a prominent Roman general and administrator during the reign of Emperor Domitian in the late 1st century AD. Originally of equestrian rank, Fuscus rose to prominence through his loyalty, competence, and military ambition, earning him key roles in both civil and military matters of the empire.

He first made his mark during the civil wars of 69 AD, the so-called *Year of the Four Emperors*, siding with Vespasian against Emperor Vitellius. His support proved crucial, and he was rewarded handsomely under the new Flavian dynasty.

By the time of Domitian's reign, Fuscus had become *Praetorian Prefect*, commanding the emperor's elite guard and serving as one of the most powerful men in Rome. In 85 AD, he was tasked with leading a punitive expedition against the Dacians, a fierce people from the region north of the Danube who had begun raiding Roman provinces.

Initially successful, Fuscus crossed the Danube and pushed deep into Dacian territory. However, in 86 AD, during an overconfident advance into the heart of enemy lands—possibly drawn by promises of Dacian gold—Fuscus fell into an ambush orchestrated by King Decebalus. The resulting disaster saw the annihilation of his legions, the loss of the legionary standards, and Fuscus himself killed in battle. His death was a humiliating blow to Rome and a personal disgrace to Domitian.

3: Cornelius Fuscus Pompeii

The plaster casts of Romans killed when Mt. Vesuvius erupted, swamping Pompeii and Herculaneum in 79 AD, are internationally famous. Scholars have long known that more people escaped the volcano's destruction of the Bay of Naples than were suffocated by it. New evidence from inscriptions provides clues to where these refugees settled.

In an open-access article in the journal *Analecta Romana*, archaeologist and historian Steven Tuck of Miami University explains how his creation of a database of Roman last names led him to match up records from Pompeii and Herculaneum, with records from the parts of Italy unaffected by the destructive power of Vesuvius.

Tuck's goal in doing this work was not just to identify refugees. He wanted *"to draw conclusions about who survived the eruption, where they relocated and why they went to certain communities. He wanted to understand what this pattern tells us about how the ancient Roman world worked socially, economically, and politically."*

In order to find refugees, Tuck needed to investigate inscriptions on public buildings and tombstones because historical records only emphasised the physical damage of disasters. This may seem odd to us today, as our news reports tend to centre the loss of human life as the main result of a catastrophe. In Roman times, only a handful of narratives, such as Pliny the Younger's account of his famous uncle's death near Pompeii, reflect the human toll of these ancient natural disasters.

An example Tuck presents comes from Roman Dacia, an area of the empire that is now Romania and Serbia. On a tombstone there dated to 87 AD, an inscription lists one Cornelius Fuscus, who was a citizen at Pompeii, lived at Neapolis, and was stationed in Dacia as a Praetorian Prefect who led five legions in Domitian's war. Fuscus *"seems to have resettled from Pompeii to Neapolis after the eruption."*

Tuck's combination of history and archaeology has produced strong evidence that it is possible to trace Vesuvian refugees. He finds that many refugees settled on the north side of the Bay of Naples, and that families tended to move together and then to marry within their refugee community. These people probably *"represent either those who fled at the first sign of the eruption,"* Tuck says, *"or those who were away from the cities when the eruption occurred."* But while this method seems to work for identifying reasonably wealthy citizens, Tuck knows that it is limited because it cannot help him discover non-Romans, slaves, or migrants who escaped Vesuvius.

4: Emperors Relating to Draco Dawn

Vespasian (r. 69–79 AD)

- Full Name: Titus Flavius Vespasianus

- Came to power after the chaos of the *Year of the Four Emperors.*

- Founder of the Flavian dynasty.

- Known for:

    - Restoring stability to Rome after Nero's fall.

    - Beginning construction of the Colosseum.

    - Tax reforms (including the infamous urine tax).

- Humble Origins: First emperor from an equestrian family (non-patrician).

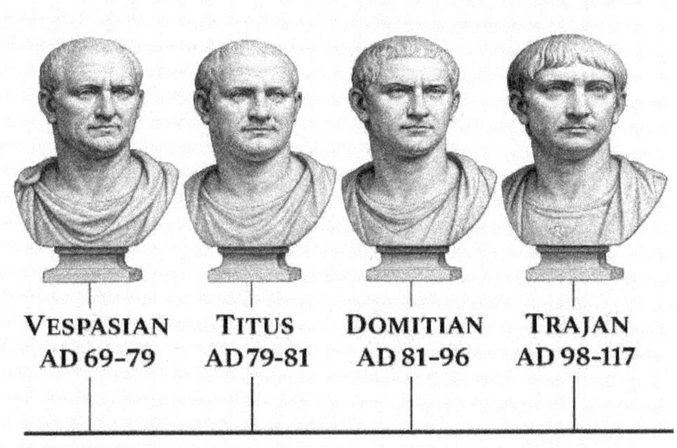

Titus (r. 79–81 AD)

- Full Name: Titus Flavius Vespasianus (son of Vespasian)

- Military Fame: Led the siege and destruction of Jerusalem in 70 AD (resulting in the *Arch of Titus*).

- Popular Emperor: Despite fears he'd be a second Nero, he was beloved for his generosity.

    - Major Events: Eruption of Mount Vesuvius in 79 AD, Pompeii

    - Completion and dedication of the Colosseum.

- Died young and mysteriously—some suspect poisoning by Domitian.

Domitian (r. 81–96 AD)

- Full Name: Titus Flavius Domitianus
- Younger brother of Titus, last of the Flavian emperors.
- Autocratic Style: Expanded emperor's power, promoted himself as a divine ruler.
- Known for:
    - Reforming the Roman currency.
    - Massive building campaigns in Rome.
    - Persecution of philosophers and Christians.
- Assassinated in a palace conspiracy; senate damned his memory (damnatio memoriae).

Nerva (r. 96–98 AD)

- Came to power after Domitian's assassination.
- First of the *Five Good Emperors.*
- Known for:

- Ending tyranny of Domitian's reign.

- Adopting Trajan to secure military loyalty.

- Short reign, mostly about stabilising power.

Trajan (r. 98–117 AD)

- Full Name: Marcus Ulpius Traianus

- First non-Italian emperor (born in Hispania).

- Known as one of the *'Five Good Emperors.'*

- Military legacy:

  - Conquered Dacia (modern Romania), adding vast wealth to Rome.

  - Trajan's Column commemorates his campaigns.

- Social Reforms: Major builder of public infrastructure (roads, aqueducts, baths).

- By his death, Rome had reached its greatest territorial extent.

5: King Decebalus Dacian Ruler

Decebalus (c. 87–106 CE)

His actual full name is unknown; *Decebalus* is likely a throne name meaning 'the Brave' or 'Strong One.'

Background

- King of Dacia (modern-day Romania and Moldova) from around 87 CE until his death in 106 CE.

- Rose to power in a period of intense conflict with the Roman Empire.

- Remembered as a charismatic leader, fierce warrior, and skilled strategist.

Conflicts with Rome

- First Battles (Domitian's Reign):

    - In 85–88 CE, Dacian forces under Decebalus launched raids into Roman territory.

    - He defeated Roman armies sent by Emperor Domitian.

    - In 89 CE, a peace treaty was signed: Decebalus remained king but became a *client king*, receiving Roman engineers, money, and weapons.

Symbolism & Culture

- Decebalus is often depicted wearing a wolfskin headdress, symbolising Dacian spiritual power and martial pride.

- He became a national hero in Romanian history, a symbol of resistance against foreign domination.

- A massive stone sculpture of his face, 'Statue of Decebalus,' was carved on the Danube's Iron Gates in modern Romania—the tallest rock sculpture in Europe.

Legacy in Art & Memory

- Immortalised in Trajan's Column in Rome.

- Central figure in many Romanian legends and nationalist movements.

- Seen as a bridge between ancient heritage and modern identity for Romania.

The King Decebalus rock sculpture is located in Romania, near the town of Orşova, along the Danube River. It is carved into a cliff face in the Iron Gates region, which forms part of the natural border between Romania and Serbia.

Height: 40 meters, making it the tallest rock sculpture in Europe.

DECEBALUS
REX
DACIE

6: *Testudo Formation*

Testudo Formation ('Tortoise' Formation)

Origin of Name:

'*Testudo*' is Latin for tortoise, referencing how the formation resembled a tortoise shell with shields forming a protective shell on all sides.

Structure & Function

- Front Line: Soldiers held their scutum (large rectangular shield) straight ahead.

- Sides: Soldiers on the edges turned their shields outward to protect the flanks.

- Top: Inner soldiers held shields overhead, forming a roof.

- This shield-wall on all sides, including the top, provided 360° protection against arrows, javelins, and projectiles during sieges or open combat.

Usage Scenarios

1. Siege Warfare:

    - Most famously used during sieges, allowing soldiers to approach walls or siege engines while protected from above.

    - During the Siege of Jerusalem (70 CE), Roman legions used the testudo effectively to advance under heavy fire.

2. Battlefield Mobility:

- ☐ Used during advances under missile fire, particularly when crossing open ground.

- ☐ Enabled tightly disciplined Roman units to close in on enemy positions with minimal casualties.

3. Psychological Impact:

- ☐ The sight of a perfectly executed testudo could demoralise enemies by showcasing Roman discipline and unity.

Strengths

- ☐ Projectile Defense: Excellent protection from arrows, slingshots, and spears.

- ☐ Morale & Discipline: Showcased the legendary cohesion of Roman legionaries.

- ☐ Tactical Mobility: Allowed slow, steady advancement in dangerous terrain.

Weaknesses

- ☐ Limited Visibility: Reduced situational awareness; soldiers relied heavily on commands.

- ▯ Mobility Constraints: Slower movement and vulnerable to close-range melee or flanking.

- ▯ Vulnerable to Heavy Weapons: Large boulders, fire, or war machines (like battering rams or catapults) could break the formation.

Historical Sources & Iconography

- ▯ Described by ancient historians like Vegetius and Cassius Dio.

- ▯ Depicted on monuments such as Trajan's Column, especially in scenes of the Dacian Wars (101–106 CE), where Romans used the testudo to storm Dacian fortifications.

Why It Worked

- ▯ Required intense training and trust between legionaries.

- ▯ Reflected the Roman military's core principles: discipline, organisation, and adaptability.

- ▯ Could quickly form or disband the formation based on orders

7: Molossian War Dogs—Historical Facts

1. Origin

- ☐ Named after the Molossians, an ancient Greek tribe from Epirus (modern Albania/Northwest Greece).

- ☐ The breed is considered an ancestor of many modern mastiff-type dogs.

2. Physical Traits

- ☐ Large, muscular, and intimidating with powerful jaws.

- ☐ Known for their bravery, loyalty, and protective nature.

- ☐ Had a short, dense coat and a broad head—built for both offense and defense.

3. Military Use

- Used by the Greeks, Romans, and possibly earlier civilisations.

- Wore spiked or armored collars and sometimes light armour to protect them in battle.

- Deployed to charge enemy lines, guard camps, and track or subdue enemies.

4. Role in Roman Warfare

- The Romans were so impressed with Molossian dogs that they adopted and bred them.

- Used not just in battles but also for hunting large animals and as guard dogs.

5. Famous Mentions

- Aristotle praised their strength and courage.

- Virgil and Grattius referenced their use in hunting.

- Pliny the Elder wrote of their role in both combat and guarding.

6. Legacy

- Believed to be the ancestor of breeds like:

    - Neapolitan Mastiff

    - English Mastiff

    - Rottweiler

    - Cane Corso

- Their bloodline influenced many modern military and police dogs in both appearance and temperament.

7. In the Arena

- Occasionally used in Roman amphitheaters, fighting wild animals or acting in staged hunts.

- Considered as strong and fearsome as lions or boars in some ancient texts.

8: The Aquila - Roman Eagle Standard

The Roman eagle standard, known as the *aquila*, was one of the most important symbols of the Roman legions.

Aquila (Eagle Standard) Facts

- Symbolism: The eagle (aquila) symbolised Rome's power, strength, and immortality.

- Material: Usually crafted from bronze or silver, sometimes gilded.

- Placement: Mounted atop a staff, carried by a specially designated soldier called the aquilifer or aquilifer (specifically for the eagle).

- Legion Identity: Each legion had its own eagle. Losing it was a massive disgrace.

- Sacred Role: The aquila was almost worshipped—shrines were dedicated to it in the legionary camps.

- Guarded Closely: It never left the legion unless they were marching or in battle.

- Shape & Style: Typically a winged eagle with outstretched wings, often clutching thunderbolts, perched on top of the pole.

END

ABOUT THE AUTHOR

Colin Dean writes with the grit of a legionary and the soul of a storyteller. A student of Roman history, Colin blends sharp historical detail with fast-paced fiction to bring the empire's darkest frontiers to life. His characters bleed, fight, and survive in stories that echo the clash of steel and the weight of loyalty.

With a passion for ancient tactics, forgotten battles, and the men who shaped history, Colin delivers stories as unforgiving as the campaigns they depict.